HAUNTED
LIVERPOOL 19

For Jan Ord

© Tom Slemen 2012

Published by The Bluecoat Press, Liverpool
Book design by March Graphic Design Studio, Liverpool
Printed by Martins the Printers

ISBN 9781908457103

Tom Slemen

HAUNTED
LIVERPOOL 19

THE BLUECOAT PRESS

CONTENTS

THE VENGEFUL SPINSTER

The following story is true in every respect; no names or places have been changed.

Many years ago in the 1970s, nineteen-year-old Des from Woolton began to see seventeen-year-old Debbie from Childwall (whose surname, as we will find out, was very unusual). One gloriously uplifting summer's day, at around 1.30pm, Des first spotted Debbie walking up Hartsbourne Avenue dressed in a white tee shirt featuring a yellow smiley face and a short bottle green skirt. On her feet she wore no socks, just a pair of Dunlop tennis shoes. Her long golden hair was stirred by a zephyr, and to Des's eyes she was a wonderful sight to behold. He asked her the time, and Debbie said, 'It's round half one now, I think.'

'Where are you going?' Des asked, walking alongside of the girl.

'To my friend's,' Debbie answered meekly, blushing slightly.

'Can I walk with you?' Des asked, cheekily.

There was a pause as Debbie's greenish blue eyes looked away. Then she said, 'If you want.'

A week later the couple were kissing in the back row of the Abbey Cinema, and after the film had ended at 10.20pm, Des started pestering Debbie to have sex with him. She kept saying no, but even as they walked along hand in hand, Des was consciously steering her towards Trinity churchyard in Wavertree's Fir Lane, where he intended to carry out the act he had dreamt of each night ever since he had met Debbie. The girl relented when Des said to her, 'I thought we had something really special, Debbie. I love you so much and want to marry you as soon as I get a job.'

They embraced, and as they did so there was an out-of-season roll of thunder in the heavens. The sweet scent of flowers on the graves created an atmosphere laden with desire. Des led Debbie into the churchyard and here, he laid her out on one of the old long gravestones that lay flat against the ground.

'I'm a virgin,' Debbie whispered timidly, but Des just said,

'Shush!' and smothered her face with passionate kisses.

As Des made love to his girlfriend, lightning flashed through the summer skies, and then as the thunder roared, the ground vibrated with so much force, Debbie had strange mental images of the dead being shaken out of their graves. She felt so much pain and yet so much pleasure as she lay there, but a few minutes into their lovemaking, heavy rain began to fall, soaking them both to the bone. Debbie felt her open mouth filling up with the rain, and she tried to push Des off.

There was a purple flash of light, and in that millisecond, Debbie saw someone standing over Des, looking over his left shoulder. The figure was of a woman with a shock of white wiry straw-like hair, and her eyes were wide and bulging, a green greyish colour with no pupils, and her jaw looked skeletal. Debbie continued to try and push Des off her when she saw the figure, but at that moment he cried out and pinned her down with tremendous strength. His hands left red marks on the sensitive skin around her wrists, and after a minute, he got to his feet, adjusted his trousers and walked off, leaving Debbie stretched out on the grave. She started to cry. What a fool she had been, all his promises of undying love had been nothing but sweet-talk. She picked herself up and straightened out her clothes and then shouted Des's name. He stopped, delved into his pocket, and treated himself to the last cigarette from a crumpled packet. He lit up, puffed on the cigarette, and said to Debbie, 'Well, what did you think?'

Debbie swore at him and called him a callous bastard. 'You just used me,' she sobbed. 'I thought you loved me.'

'I do love you, you stupid get,' Des told her, then climbed over the short railings and stormed off in a huff.

Sobbing, Debbie tried to follow him, but almost fell as she clambered over the railings. She walked home to Childwall, soaked through and feeling angry and hurt. The emptiness she felt inside and the cold temporarily blotted out the memory of that strange ghoulish figure she had seen looming over her and Des in the graveyard. As Debbie reached Childwall Valley Road, she heard running behind her, and turned to see that it was Des with a smile on his face. 'I've been shouting you ever since you crossed over Church Road, didn't you hear me, deaf lugs?'

Debbie walked on, head in the air, trying to look as if she wasn't bothered.

'Debbie, I love you, girl, stop being like this!' Des caught up and seized her forearm.

Debbie slapped his hand and pulled her arm away. 'You're really horrible, and you couldn't even do it properly!' she said, marching along as the thunder rolled again.

'Well that's because you're a virgin!' Des shouted, and stopped in his tracks. He followed this up with a string of insults as she walked off into the night. Debbie put the sorry episode down to experience; this was to be just the first encounter with the many male scumbags she would encounter in her life, all out for one thing, and it certainly wasn't romance. She felt as if her innocence had been robbed.

That night, Des watched the television until around midnight, and when his parents went to bed, he sneaked into the hallway and stole a few cigarettes from the box of twenty Embassy in his father's inside coat pocket. He then lay in bed, smoking and listening to the *Night Owl* music programme on Radio City. He thought about his escapade in the cemetery, and then he dozed off. Des woke around 3am, and opened the window. It was sweltering in the bedroom – the storm had done nothing to lessen the humid summer air. He took off his underpants and lay under just a thin nylon sheet. He quickly drifted off into the strange territory of dreams, and had one of the worst nightmares in his life. A skeletal naked woman with a shock of white hair was stretched out on the ceiling above Des's bed, and her saliva was drooling out of her open mouth and falling in vile strings on to his face. Then she let out an ear-splitting scream and fell from the ceiling on to him. As she landed on him, he was forced to examine her face close up, and was struck by the fact that her eyes had no pupils. They were bulging like hard-boiled eggs, stripped of their shells, with a greenish-grey tinge to them. The old hag began to utter the most disgusting obscenities and told Des she was about to make love to him. Des screamed and tried to force her off him, but the zombie-like woman just laughed and said: 'I'm a virgin too! Yes, you despicable little [expletive deleted]! Make love to me or I'll claw your eyes out!'

And her bony skeletal fingers began to fondle Des's face. She had long thick dirty fingernails, and they clawed at Des's right cheek, drawing blood. Her other cold claw-like hand was sliding down past the teenager's navel. Try as he might, Des could not push the living corpse off him, and somehow she managed to start making love to him. He felt her bristly tongue snaking around inside his mouth and when it touched his tonsils he almost threw up. The woman started to shake and scream with manic laughter, and the two of them rolled over in a hideous embrace – and fell off the bed.

Des woke up, startled, with thunder booming in the skies outside. The curtains were blowing wildly in the stormy wind. He shuddered as he recalled the old hag, then got back into bed, so relieved that it had all been a dream, but then he felt something trickle down his right cheek like a tear. It was blood. He stroked the wetness and looked at the blood on his middle fingertip, then realised the old hag could not have been a dream, and he felt the end of the bed move as if someone was still there. In the semi-darkness he saw her squatting there on all fours. Her bare breasts hanging, triangular and deflated, and even in the poor light he could see the saliva drooling from the open mouth on to the bed cover.

Des ducked under the thin blanket and screamed for his mother and father as the ghoul pounced. She shrieked with laughter as she tore into the blankets, shredding them with her powerful soil-encrusted nails, ripping the fabric apart and inflicting wounds on Des's arms, legs and torso. The attack seemed to go on for ever, until the light came on in the bedroom, and Des felt the sheet being torn off his bed. His mother stood there with a look of sheer horror on her face as she saw her naked son laying there, his face and body lacerated all over with red glistening scratches. 'Des, what … oh my God!' she gasped, and then his father came into the room.

No one could explain what had happened. Des's father said he had heard of foxes getting into houses and inflicting injuries to children, but such a fox would have to negotiate the stairs to reach Des's bedroom, after gaining entry into the house, but how, as there were no open windows on the ground floor. Des's mother wondered if some kind of bobcat – a wild feral feline – had managed to climb in through his open window, but she quickly dismissed the idea. In the end, she decided that a maniac must have shinned up the drainpipe outside to get into the bedroom to attack her son, perhaps with some kind of knife.

But Des felt the old hag had visited him because of his callous behaviour in the cemetery, and he recalled the words she said about her being a 'virgin too' – just like Debbie. When he met Debbie a few weeks later, he told her about the ghoulish woman who had attacked him in his bed, and with great delight, Debbie told him what she had seen in the cemetery that night as Des had his wicked way with her, and Des shivered. Debbie then added that she was now seeing someone else and that he was much better at love-making than Des. Des refused to sleep in his room after that night, and slept instead in a spare room surrounded by copious quantities of holy water, crucifixes and a large old leather-bound edition of the Bible. These seemed to do the trick, and he suffered no further encounters with the old hag.

Des's story soon did the rounds in Woolton, and came to the attention of local investigator into the paranormal, John Finnegan, who asked Des to show him the gravestone on which he had made love to Debbie. Des could not be sure exactly which gravestone it was, but narrowed it down to a row of three. John researched the names on the gravestones and made a chilling discovery: Debbie, having a very unusual surname, was undoubtedly a descendant of a woman who had been buried in one of the graves that Des had pointed out. The woman with the same surname as Debbie had died late in her life, and had never married. The sisters of this woman had all married and had children, but this particular woman had died a spinster. When Des discovered this, he bought a huge bunch of flowers and placed it on the grave and said a prayer, in which he asked Debbie's ancestor to forgive him, and after that day, Des also began to attend church each Sunday.

SAY WHO YOU ARE

The Liverpool district of Fazakerley has the distinction of having a unique place name; there is nowhere else in the country with that name, and the meaning and origin of the name Fazakerley remains a mystery. The ancient Fazakerleigh family took their name from the district, and speculated that the name might be Anglo-Saxon, but this doesn't seem to be the case. Fazakerley is not only a name of mysterious origins, the whole district is one of the most haunted on Merseyside, and the following story is just one tale about the supernatural goings-on in the area.

Just a stone's throw from University Hospital Aintree, there is a certain Fazakerley factory which has kept going through thick and thin, through boom-time and recession, and of course, most factories have a security guard or two, and this factory had two men whom we shall call Greg and Nick, both in their thirties. Nick had been a guard at the factory for almost four years in 2002, and had quite a chequered work history. He had worked in a casino in Turkey, then left to be a farm labourer in the south of France for a few years, before gradually gravitating back to his home town of Liverpool, where he found work as a doorman on a city centre club. After sustaining a few violent attacks by coked-up club goers, Nick opted for a quieter job at the Fazakerley factory, and found the nocturnal hours rather conducive and beneficial to his state of mind. Nick would read books he had wanted to study for years, and sometimes listened to Classic FM between doing his rounds. Greg was a rather brash, in-your-face type of character, the type who could cadge money from a bailiff, but it was understood that he would never try to invade Nick's bubble of personal space or try and order him about – even though Greg was a few years older than his colleague and had been a guard for 15 years.

It was a Friday morning at 2.30am. Greg did his rounds at the factory, and when he came back to the office, which was basically just a glorified garden hut at the end of a huge yard dotted with crates, he saw Nick doing *The Times* crossword. 'God, it's a bit King

Billy out there.'

'Bit what?' Nick asked without looking up from the newspaper.

'Chilly,' moaned Greg, 'Chilli beans.'

'Just made some coffee for you,' Nick said, and he nodded to the cluttered desk then tapped the top of his Parker pen against his bottom lip as he dwelt on the cryptic clue to a twelve-letter word with three U's in it.

'Ta,' replied Greg, and he grabbed the large black ceramic mug of hot Nescafé, took a sip, then located an unopened packet of custard creams. Greg dunked one biscuit after another and slurped the coffee, and Nick finally said, 'Can you stop that?'

'Stop what?' Greg asked, perplexed.

'Slurping,' Nick snapped, and shook his head as he filled in the wrong squares in the crossword.

'Is it okay if I breathe?' asked Greg, 'Or does that get on your nerves as well?'

'Listen!' Nick looked beyond the panes of the office out into the blackness of the yard.

'What?' Greg followed his gaze, and looked out into the yard.

'Can you hear it?' Nick put the newspaper and ballpoint down and went to the door. He opened the door, admitting an icy breeze, then looked out into the blackness. 'Here!' he said to Greg, 'Listen!'

Greg came to the doorway slurping the coffee.

'Sssh!' Nick put his index finger to his lips and then he said, 'Can you hear it?'

The two guards stood in silence, and sure enough, in the midst of the faint howling of the wind around the crates and high walls of the yard, they both heard someone singing.

'I can hear it,' Greg said, and yawned. 'It's a radio somewhere in the distance.'

Nick shook his head twice. 'It's not a radio, that's someone singing, but where's it coming from?'

'Sound travels further at night,' Greg explained, and his eyes darted about because the singing voice sounded eerie.

'What is that song?' Nick tilted his head so his good ear – his right one – faced the end of the yard.

Greg squinted as the wind buffeted his eyes. 'Seal,' he suddenly said.

Nick's eyes became animated and he gave a slight smile. 'Yeah, that's it; that song by Seal. *Kiss From a Rose.*'

'I've been kissed by a rose on the grey …' Greg tried to sing a line from the song.

But the singer was not singing those words, and as the two guards listened in the dead of night, the unknown vocalist suddenly belted out a strange version which went: 'I've been kissed by a rose on the grave …'

'He's making his own words up now,' said Nick, with a nervous laugh, because the mention of a grave at that time in the morning was very unsettling. And the singing stopped dead. Just the wind was moaning now, and suddenly a huge moth flew into the office and hit Greg in his left eye – and the guard had a terrible phobia about moths, especially overgrown velvet-winged ones with golden bug eyes. Greg let out a yelp and tried to hurl the hot coffee over the fluttering stout-bodied insect as it circled his head, but the coffee just missed Nick and went out into the yard. Nick picked up his copy of *The Times* and batted the moth out into the night and slammed the door. Greg shuddered and when he rolled up his sleeves and went to the sink to wash his eye, Nick could see the goosepimples raised on his forearms.

At a quarter to four, another sinister sound was heard by the two guards; the sound of a spade, digging into stony soil. This time, Greg heard the unusual sound first and drew Nick's attention to it. They opened the office door. Nick was due to do his rounds in ten minutes and seemed quite nervous. He listened in the yard, and once again, he heard that song again with its twisted lyrics, and the sound of a shovel digging away, spading earth. Nick swore under his breath, then went to a cupboard and got a new battery out and fitted it to his torch. He also located his old MagLite torch in his locker and was glad to see it still had some power in it.

'I've never seen you like this,' Greg said to his colleague. 'You look all on edge. It's just sound travelling through the night, echoing, probably from miles away.'

Nick didn't even reply. He put on his coat, looked at the screen of his mobile to see if the battery was in need of charging, and as usual its indicator showed it only had 14 per cent power left. The walkie-talkie was switched on, and Nick whistled a random tune to take his mind off the situation.

'Do you want me to go round with you?' Greg asked.

'Nah, it's okay, I'm not that scared, mate,' Nick told him and smirked, but Greg could tell his friend was very unnerved by the strange sounds they'd both heard.

'There it is again,' Greg said, holding his hand out with his index finger pointing upwards. 'Be a laugh if someone was tunnelling in here.'

'Wouldn't be a laugh,' Nick said, and he went to the door. 'See you in a mo.' He left the office and walked down the long dark yard and into the labyrinth of walkways between towering stacks of crates, portakabins and pallets. At the very bottom of the yard, he turned left, with both torches shining the way, and here he could hear that creepy singer quite clearly, and Nick could literally feel the hairs on the back of his neck rising up.

'I've been kissed by a rose on a grave ...'

Then he saw the singer. He wasn't sure if it was a he or a she, because all he could see was a shadowy figure, and it was either the silhouette of a nun or someone wearing a hood and the cowl of a monk, but they were close up to a wire-link fence, and even when the two torchbeams were aimed at the figure, Nick could see nothing but blackness in it, as if he was shining a torch down a bottomless pit. He was so afraid of the weird 'thing' he could hardly breathe, and when Greg's voice came across the walkie-talkie, joking about ghosts, Nick couldn't even reply. The guard turned on his heels and walked back the way he had come with the sounds of his heart pounding through his carotid artery. When he got back to the office, he said to Greg, 'There's something all in black by the fence.'

'What?' Greg could see that all the colour had drained from his colleague's face.

Nick realised he still had the torches on and he switched them off as he gave a garbled reply. 'There's a thing, all in black, like a monk or a nun, in a long robe, and its just all shadow, by the wire fence.'

'Shurrup!' Greg said, thinking – or hoping – that Nick was pulling his leg.

'I swear on our Michael's life,' Nick said, referring to his three-year-old son, 'there's a ghost out there. It was singing, and I could hear that sound of a spade digging dead clear when I got by it.'

Greg suddenly turned towards the window panes of the office and swore loudly.

Nick turned to see what he was swearing at – and there it was – the thing he had seen by the fence a few minutes ago. It was moving out of the darkness up the yard, only visible because it contrasted against a block of light-coloured crates. The thing moved as if it was on wheels, slowly but steadily towards the office. 'That's it!' Nick said, and he looked at Greg's face. He had never seen his friend so scared in all the time he'd worked with him. Greg had tackled an intruder at the factory once in the bravest manner, even though the prowler had a knife, but this was different – it was something unearthly – and that terrified them both.

The shadowy creature halted about thirty feet away. Greg found his high-powered lantern torch and shone it at the figure, lighting up the yard, and Nick shone his two torches, but still the guards could see not one bit of detail within the entity. It was pure blackness, as dark as the interior of a coffin.

Greg suddenly picked up his mobile and started to dial.

'Who you calling?' Nick asked.

Greg didn't answer. He looked back through the windows at that uncanny visitor, then to the faint tinny voice on his phone he said, 'Police, police!'

Nick wasn't keen on him phoning the law because he thought they'd laugh at the idea of two guards reporting a ghost, but Greg didn't mention the ominous figure.

'Hiya. I'm a guard at a factory in Fazakerley, and there's a dangerous intruder on the premises – could you send someone round please a.s.a.p?' Greg told the woman on the police switchboard, and gave the name of the factory, his own name and the postcode of the premises.

Less than ten minutes later – and those minutes felt like hours to the guards – a blue flashing light could be seen down by the gates of the factory – but to unlock those gates, the guards would have to pass the apparition, which was still standing in the same spot, radiating pure menace. Greg estimated that it looked as if it was about five-feet-seven in height.

'We'll have to just run past it,' Nick said, opening the office door and looking down the yard with the high-beam of the lantern sweeping from left to right across the ghostly figure.

'Okay, mate,' said Greg, and the two guards ran as fast as their legs could carry them, and straight away, the black figure moved slowly towards the left – intending to intercept them, and Nick flew past it first, and then Greg passed within inches of the thing, and he thought he heard a voice cry out from it. As Nick panicked and inserted the key into the gate's padlock the wrong way round, the shadowy creature began to move down the yard towards them faster and faster.

'Hurry up!' shouted Greg, ready to climb the gate to get away from the entity if need be. Two policemen were getting out of their car about twenty feet away outside. At last the padlock clicked and Nick and Greg yanked at the gate and pulled it open. They ran to the police and said, 'Look at this thing!'

The policemen trotted to the gates and looked into the yard.

They saw nothing.

One of the policemen shone his own torch into the yard, and then he went into the yard and said, 'Where is he?'

Another police car turned up, and soon the yard was occupied by four policemen plus Greg and Nick, and when the guards described what had happened, the policemen just looked at one another without saying a word, until finally, one of the officers said, 'It's probably been a hoodie. With this bad lighting here you'd probably think you'd seen all kinds of things. You should have a floodlight down here and maybe get the bosses to stick a camera up near the front of the place.'

The police then departed, and not long afterwards, the milky pale light of dawn infiltrated the skies over the Fazakerley factory. The guards went home at 7am, and that morning at 10.15am, Greg left his bed to go the toilet, and his wife heard him scream, then shout out: 'Say who you are!' and this was followed a loud thud. She called out to her husband, then sensed something was badly wrong. She got up, hurried along the landing, and found Greg on the floor outside the toilet. He was lying there on his back with his hands clutching his chest – with his eyes wide open. He looked as if he were dead, but his wife called an ambulance, and she saw the ambulance men look grimly at one another after they had tried to resuscitate him. One of the ambulance men quickly put his index and middle fingers over Greg's eyes to close the lids. Greg's wife then let out a terrible scream. Her husband had died of a heart attack. He'd smoked forty cigarettes a day until a few months back when he took to wearing nicotine patches.

Nick never mentioned the sinister entity which had stalked him and Greg at the factory on the very morning his friend had died, and when Greg's wife said she had heard her husband cry out: 'Say who you are!' before he collapsed, Nick felt a shiver run down his spine. He wondered if that thing had paid a visit to Greg during his last moments – and had called to 'collect' him, knowing that his time was almost up.

Nick went to the funeral, and after the service, they played a recording of a song that meant a lot to Greg's wife, for she had started dating Greg in the summer of 1995 when the song was in the charts. It was Seal's *Kiss From a Rose*. Nick went stone cold inside when he heard this song, and recalled the occasion when he and his late friend had heard that song being sung by that entity during that fateful night. And Nick also recalled the sound of a spade digging. Did it symbolise the grave that was about to be dug for Greg? Greg had often talked about death in the wee small hours, and he had always told Nick that he wanted to be cremated if he 'bit the big one' – a phrase he often used about meeting his end. And yet Greg's wife had decided he would be buried for some reason.

Nick noticed all the roses on Greg's coffin as it was being was lowered into the ground forever, and immediately thought about the eerie line of that song sung by God knows what: 'kissed by a rose on a grave ...'

Understandably, Nick later handed in his notice at the factory in Fazakerley, but I have heard that the reaper-like figure is still occasionally seen in the vicinity, and in 2009, I received an email from a man who reported seeing a black hooded silhouette gliding down Sandy Lane, which is not a thousand miles away from that factory.

SOMEWHERE ONLY WE KNOW

Have you ever suddenly recollected some unusual occurrence from your childhood, then thought, did that really happen or was it something I dreamt or some memory of an incident that happened on a television programme? I recall being visited by what I can only describe as a shadow-being when I was about two. It would sneakily slide out of the wall of my bedroom, almost immediately after my mum or dad had tucked me in and I vaguely remember pressing the tip of a butter-knife against my chest after some information was imparted to me from the silhouetted being which convinced me that I'd be okay if I died 'and went back'. My mother stopped me from doing any self-injury – or even worse – just in time. I think the shadow stopped visiting me some time after that. I have had the opportunity through my unusual work to talk to many people from all walks of life about the paranormal, and a lot of folk have told me of similar recollections of some very odd things which have lain buried in their memories for years. What follows is based on the recollections of two men who are, at the time of writing, what we imprecisely term as middle-aged. See what you think.

In the summer school holidays of 1972, two ten-year-olds from

Bootle named Davy and Barry, were invited to go and stay with Barry's old Auntie Agnes, or 'Aggie' as Barry called her, at a crumbling old house on Cambridge Street, just around the corner from the Oxford Street Maternity Hospital (now converted to house a suite of apartments known as Lennon Studios, as John Lennon was born there when it was a maternity hospital, as I was myself). Davy was from a rather clean home, and was quite shocked when he saw his first cockroach at Aggie's house, crawling across the kitchen floor and he felt sick when Aggie halted in the middle of frying some sausages to stoop down and pick up the roach before tossing it out the kitchen window. When Davy told Barry about the disgusting way his auntie had continued cooking without washing her hands, Barry said, 'Don't start calling Auntie Aggie, or you'll be going home!'

Aggie was a widow who lived with her much older brother Alf, who immediately struck Davy as a rather enigmatic man who knew something. 'Knows what?' Barry asked his best friend, but Davy just said, 'I don't know, it's hard to explain. I just think he knows things.'

And that teatime, Aggie and Alf and some talkative next-door neighbour named Queenie sat with the boys around the big table, eating fish, chips and peas, when Barry said, 'Hey, Uncle Alf, Davy says you know things.'

Davy's face went pinkish-red, and he said to Barry, 'No I didn't, you!'

Barry grinned wickedly and said: 'You did, you said he knows things and you've gone all red, ha!'

'Stop talking at the table and eat your tea, Barry!' Aggie told her nephew sternly.

Barry licked the tip of his index finger and then placed it on his own face as he made a hissing sound as he pointed at red-faced Davy. 'You've gone like a tomato!'

'Hey, Barry, be quiet and leave Davy to eat his tea!' said Alf, and he smiled at Davy and winked.

After tea, Barry and Davy left the house to go gallivanting. They played with a few children of an Irish family called the Ryans who lived locally, then went to explore the rocks outside the crypt section of the Roman Catholic Cathedral, which lay just a few hundred yards away. Around 10pm, as twilight fell, Queenie could be heard shouting for Barry in a yodelling type of voice. The two boys went to Aggie's house, and they were treated to cordial, jelly and cream, and then told to go upstairs to share the bath. The boys sat in the bath with their underpants on, flicking water and hurtling Crazy Bath Foam at one another, until Aggie came in and told them to get dry and go to bed immediately. The boys did, and had to share an old double bed in a room with mildewed wallpaper and old fashioned furniture. Just after midnight, Davy and Barry were still awake, and telling one another stories, when Barry decided to go and root about in an ancient-looking mahogany cabinet. The two doors of the cabinet were adorned with what antique dealers would describe as foliate fretwork panels. Barry knelt down, opened the doors, and looked inside at the bundles of old yellowed newspapers. He shifted the bundles out of the way and found another door set into the back of the cabinet, and so he turned the handle to reveal a small flight of steps that disappeared down into darkness. 'Wow! Look at this, Davy! It's a secret passage.'

Davy got out of bed and went to see what his friend was talking about. When he saw the steps, he had a bad feeling about the discovery, and advised Barry to close the inner door and put the newspapers back in place, but Barry was already crawling into the cabinet towards the stairs. 'Don't, Barry, you might fall down a hole down there!' Davy warned, and then he saw an old candle in a holder on the cabinet, and he told Barry they should light it to show the way. Barry came back out and after he and Davy had gone downstairs to the kitchen to light the candle from the pilot light on the cooker, they returned to the bedroom and went inside the cabinet. Each boy was barefooted and Barry only wore his underpants, whereas Davy had old baggy pyjama bottoms on. They descended the ice-cold sandstone steps and came to a number of doors of different shapes and sizes. Barry carefully opened the first door, which was only about one-and-a-half feet high and two feet across, and the boys found themselves looking down at someone's parlour. An old woman was asleep in a high-backed chair in front of a fire, and her cat on the fireside rug was gazing up at the boys, who began to giggle. 'Whose house is this?' Barry asked and sniggered. The old woman started to snore, and Barry shouted: 'Hey, love!' startling the poor old thing. And then he slammed the door shut and went to look at the other doors. 'We should go back now,' Davy said nervously, his hand cupped around the candle, guarding it from draughts.

'No, this is great!' said Barry excitedly, and he pulled open a bigger door which was about three feet square to reveal a tunnel. The boys crawled down the tunnel and saw light streaming from a square on the wall which turned out to be a ventilator grille. They looked through it and saw a woman, aged about forty or less, sitting in the bath, reading a book. Davy was terrified of being caught as some Peeping Tom, and tried to back away on his knees, but Barry put his fingers to his mouth and whistled loudly through the ventilator, startling the woman. The boys heard an almighty splash and the woman shouted: 'Who's that? Who's there?'

The boys returned to the steps which led to the cabinet and fled up them to the bedroom. The inner cabinet door was slammed shut and the bundles of newspapers were put back in place. The boys laughed about their bizarre discovery until well after 1am, and then they both fell fast asleep. The next morning when they awoke they agreed not to mention the secret passage and the doors and tunnels to anyone. As the boys sat at the table for a breakfast of boiled eggs and fried bread, Aggie said to them, 'What was all that racket about in your room last night, eh?'

'Wasn't us, Auntie,' Barry replied with a slight telltale grin on his face, 'we went to sleep straight away.'

'Well the bugs must have clogs on in this house then,' Aggie replied with a shake of the head.

That evening at 7pm, Alf gave Barry and Davy a drawing pad each and some felt tip pens. The boys said they were going upstairs to their room to draw a comic strip, but this was just a pretence to go and explore the tunnels leading from the cabinet once again. On this occasion, the boys travelled some distance down a tunnel until they came to a normal-sized door, and when they opened it, they found themselves in a room lined with expensive-looking leather-bound books. The carpet was dark red, and from the ceiling hung an elaborate crystal chandelier. The boys entered the room and went to another door, and from behind this door came the most peculiar-sounding music they had ever heard. It sounded just like a piano playing a tune in reverse. 'Let's go, quick, come on, Barry,' Davy whispered as he watched his over-intrepid friend reach for the door handle.

Barry turned the handle, and there was a man sitting at a grand piano dressed in a black coat with hammer tails. His face looked very strange. He had a long aquiline nose, bulging eyes with dark circles around them, and protuberant teeth which stuck out as he grinned. He was hammering the keys with his hands and making an unholy racket. All of a sudden, the odd-looking pianist happened to glance over at the door, and he spotted Barry spying in on him. He stopped playing, leapt to his feet, and ran towards the boys. Davy was out of the library like a shot, and was soon scrambling back along the tunnel to the flight of steps. He heard Barry's screams echoing behind him and a man's gruff voice. Davy fell out of the cabinet and ran downstairs to tell Aggie what had happened but he collided with Barry's Uncle Alf on the bottom step.

'Hey! What's all this?' Alf said, leaning against the newel post with his hands clutching his stomach where Davy's head had winded him.

Davy rattled off an almost incoherent attempt at explanation of what had just occurred and Alf ran up to the room, followed by Davy, who took slow, reluctant steps to reach the bedroom. When Davy entered the bedroom it was empty, and the cabinet door was wide open. He could hear Alf arguing with someone and the sound of Barry crying his eyes out. A few minutes later, Barry came running out of the cabinet with his shirt torn and his face slicked with grubby tears. He ran past Davy and out of the room. Then Alf came out of the cabinet on all fours with a cut lip, and without a word of explanation, he closed the inner door of the mahogany cabinet, then put all of the newspaper bundles back in place and slammed the two doors shut with quite a temper. He then pushed Davy out of the room and said, 'You're going home!'

Down in the kitchen there was a blazing row between Alf and Aggie. 'They're nothing but trouble and they're going home tonight, so help me God!' bawled Alf.

'Over my dead body they are!' countered Aggie, and she hugged a sobbing Barry and said, 'Stop crying, pet, you and your friend are staying here! Take no notice of your uncle!'

Alf stormed off out of the house but later returned and remained sulkily silent for an hour. After supper, the boys went up to their room and Davy asked Barry what had happened when the man who had been playing the piano had caught him. Barry said he had tried to bite his arms and legs but he had punched him and hit him with a chair, and Barry had hidden under the piano at one point, but then Uncle Alf came upon the scene and the two men started to punch one another. As Barry was telling all this to an engrossed Davy, three raps sounded on the double doors of the mahogany cabinet, and Davy let out a yelp and sat up in bed, eyes fixed on the source of the sounds. The doors opened, and a boy of around seven or eight stepped out. He wore a dirty pale shirt with no collar and a pair of trousers that ended just under the knees. He blinked at Davy and Barry from the interior of the cabinet, and then he and Barry posed the same question simultaneously: 'Who are you?' they said.

Barry got out the bed and stooped down to look past the stranger in case that man was around, but the boy was alone.

'I'm Billy,' said the boy.

'Where are you from, Billy?' Barry asked him.

'From in there,' Billy said, pointing into the dark passageway behind him.

'Do you know who that man is who plays the piano?' Barry queried.

'Mr Wroot plays the piano,' said Billy, 'and he's trying to kill me.'

'Trying to kill you?' said Davy, feeling very unsafe all of a sudden.

'You'd better come in here then,' Barry advised Billy, and the young boy came into the bedroom and Barry went into one of the drawers in the dresser and found a pair of old brown nylon stockings that must have belonged to Aggie. He used one of the stockings to tie together the door handles of the mahogany cabinet – just in case Mr Wroot should try and get into the room.

'Do you live next door?' Davy asked Billy, and the boy returned a puzzled expression.

'No, in there,' and Billy nodded towards the cabinet.

'Yeah, we know you came out there, but where's your house?' Barry asked. 'Is it in this street? Who made all those secret passages?'

Billy shrugged. 'I don't know. I live in there; that's where I live.'

'You can stay here if you like,' Barry told Billy, and pointed to the bed.

Billy nodded enthusiastically and soon the three boys were sitting on the bed, and Davy was showing Billy how to draw with the felt tips. Billy seemed fascinated by the pens, and was equally mesmerised by the bedside lamp, and burnt his fingers twice touching the bulb. At half-past one in the morning, there came a gentle tapping on the doors of the cabinet, and all three boys awoke with a start. Billy was sleeping at the bottom of the bed, top-tail fashion to the other two. He sat up with a look of fear on his face and stared at the cabinet doors, which were bulging now as someone behind them pushed against them. Then a smooth-sounding voice, laden with menace, said, 'Billy? Are you in there?'

Billy recoiled with a yelping sound and backed away from the cabinet until he was sitting between Davy and Barry.

'Is that him?' Davy whispered to Billy. 'Is that Mr Wroot?'

Billy was so afraid of the man behind those doors, he never heard Davy's question, and Barry, seeing how terrified the boy was, led him out of the room. All three went downstairs to the kitchen, where Barry armed himself with a huge carving knife, and Davy grabbed the heavy cast iron poker from the fire grate.

Billy started to sniffle, and tears rolled from his eye as he trembled uncontrollably.

'Don't be scared, Billy, he won't get you, I promise,' Barry tried to

24

reassure his new friend. 'Davy and I will kill him.'

All of a sudden, there came the sound of movement behind the kitchen walls, and the boys froze as they realised that Wroot must be using some hidden passages leading to the kitchen. They heard loose powdery plaster behind the damp wallpaper trickling down, and it sounded like sand falling on the skin of a drum.

'He's here!' little Billy sobbed, looking about at the walls.

Davy and Barry were speechless with fear and confusion. How could this man track their movements around the house behind the walls?

A deadly silence descended, and the only sound to be heard came from cats hissing and screeching at one another in the distance somewhere. Then the door of the cupboard under the sink flew open and that man Davy had seen playing the piano in that secret room – the one who had captured Barry and tried to bite him on the arms and legs – reached out and with his large hand grabbed Billy by his left ankle. Before Billy could even cry out, Mr Wroot yanked at his ankle and the boy fell forwards and cracked his forehead on the hard tiles as he fell face down. Billy was knocked clean out by the fall, and Wroot laughed as his other arm reached out and seized the other ankle of the unconscious boy.

'No!' Barry screamed. He wanted to stab Wroot but was too afraid to even try, and he and Davy watched in horror as the little boy was dragged into the cupboard under the sink. Wroot closed the door behind him, and then Barry and Davy heard the maniac move behind the wall as he returned to what was presumably his lair.

The door of the kitchen burst open, and Davy let out a scream. Aggie came in wearing a hairnet and nightgown, followed by Alf, who was wearing red and white striped pyjamas. 'What's all this noise, eh?' Aggie yelled, her eyes all bloodshot.

Barry opened the cupboard door under the sink and pointed to the cylinder of Vim and bottles of disinfectant and Windolene laying on their sides in disarray. He spouted out the story of Billy coming out of the cabinet on the run from a Mr Wroot, at which point Alf stopped the boy's conversation stone dead by shouting at him to: 'Stop!'

'Come on you two, get to bed!' Aggie hollered at Barry and Davy. 'And you can put that knife back in the drawer,' she said to Barry, at the same time taking the poker from Davy's grip.

The boys begrudgingly went back upstairs to their room, and Davy whispered to Barry: 'I want to go home in the morning, I've had enough of this.'

'But we can't go home and leave Billy with that man,' Barry told his friend, recalling the way he had tried to sink his teeth into him when he captured him in that room.

'I don't care about Billy, I hate this house!' Davy confessed.

At a quarter to four in the morning, the boys awoke from their very light sleep, and heard distant screams. Alf knocked on the wall and shouted, 'I won't warn you two again!'

'It isn't us!' Barry shouted to the wall.

'Get to sleep now!' Alf cried out.

'Those screams;' Davy whispered, and his eyes seemed full of terror now; 'they sounded like Billy's screams.'

'We've got to help him,' said Barry, and he said this three times to Davy and elicited three shakes of Davy's head. 'Well I'm helping him!' Barry said, and he sneaked out of the room again and took ages tiptoeing down the stairs, avoiding the creaky steps, until he reached the kitchen, where he looked for some candles. He was terrified because he imagined that Wroot would emerge from some cupboard at any moment and seize him in a flash, but he managed to obtain two candles and some matches before sneaking at a snail's pace back up the stairs to the room. He undid the stockings on the door handles of the mysterious mahogany cabinet and removed the newspaper bundles. The silver handle on the inner door was turned and the two boys bravely went in search of little Billy.

They tried the door that led to that library, where the man they assumed to be Wroot attacked Barry, but it was locked. The duo tried another door, and looked in on the darkened parlour where they had seen the old woman dozing in the high-backed chair, but there was no sign of the woman, and the chiming of the clock on the mantelpiece striking the hour of four startled the boys. On the way back down the passage, Davy noticed a peephole in the door to the locked library, but it was too high up for either boy to look through, so he bent over and rested his hands on his kneecaps as Barry stood on his back, using him as a human step. Barry steadied himself, and looked through the hole. What he saw was so horrific, so shocking, he fell from Davy's back and ran off, unable to speak or cry out, leaving his candle in the holder on the floor.

'Wait for me!' Davy shouted after his terror-stricken friend, and he had the good sense to pick Barry's candle up off the floor before he ran after him. When Davy reached the bedroom he found it empty, and he heard a commotion downstairs. When Davy went down to the hallway he came upon Barry in tears, lit by the light shining through the doorway of the parlour. In the doorframe, silhouetted, stood the boy's Uncle Alf with his coat on over his pyjamas, and he roared: 'Enough is enough! As soon as it's light, you two pests are out of here and I don't care what Aggie says this time! You could have caused a fire going round the place with candles at all hours in the morning! Now get back to bed!'

And he lurched towards Davy, who backed away in fright. Alf snatched the candles from each of the boy's hands and told him to get to bed. 'Pronto! Go on! Get up there!' he barked.

Up in the room, Davy asked his friend what he had seen through the peephole, and as Barry tied not one, but three stockings around the handles of the mahogany cabinet, he started to sniffle again.

'What did you see?' Davy pressed his friend, but soon wished he hadn't asked him.

Barry knelt there after tying the third knot of the stockings, and said: 'That weird man was sitting at a table, and he had one of those things tied round his neck under his chin ...'

'You mean a napkin?' Davy asked.

Barry nodded, and tears came streaming down his face. 'And there was all blood on it, and he had a knife and a fork and on the plate was ... was ... Billy's head ...' Barry started to cry again, and he buried his face in his hands.

Uncle Alf started knocking on the wall, and faint cries of: 'Shut up and get to sleep!' could be heard through the thin wall.

'What? Billy's head?' Davy recoiled in horror. A nervous twitch played in his cheek.

'He'd cut his nose off and he had it on the end of the fork, and Billy's eyes were gone as well ...' Barry's voice trailed off into a whisper.

'Why would he do that to Billy?' Davy began to shake, and he looked at the cabinet then backed away and sat on the end of the bed – the end furthest away from that deadly portal to a very strange world of tunnels, doors and strange characters.

'Listen!' Barry suddenly said, and his eyes widened and turned right towards the bound doors of the cabinet.

Davy tried to stop breathing so he could listen more intently. Yes, he could hear it too. That peculiar piano and its odd-sounding music was playing faintly. Wroot was tinkling the ivories.

'Maybe we should leave,' Barry suggested, and Davy nodded enthusiastically.

The faint piano music stopped.

'How can we get home though?' Barry pondered, 'Bootle's miles away.'

'We should go to the police and tell them about Billy, and they'll lock that man up,' Davy said, still shaking from that mental image of Billy's severed head on the plate with no eyes and the bloody napkin and carved-off nose.

There came faint footsteps on the stairs outside. Barry and Davy looked at one another – two pallid faces barely visible in the bedroom, where the only light came from an old sodium light burning outside in the entry. 'Who's that?' Davy whispered.

The footfalls halted outside the bedroom door. The floor creaked outside that door.

Davy went to the dresser and picked up an old vase, ready to throw it at whoever was outside. He somehow knew – somehow sensed – that it wasn't Barry's Uncle Alf out there.

'Who is it?' Barry said to the door.

The doorhandle squeaked as it slowly turned, and the door

28

opened a few inches.

'Uncle Alf, is that you?' Barry asked, and began to blink rapidly. No reply came.

'Uncle Alf?' Barry asked once more.

'Get to bed!' came Uncle Alf's faint voice from next door. So, if Alf was in bed, who was coming into the room?

The door opened steadily and Barry and Davy backed away to the other side of the room, near to the window.

That man – the cannibal who had been seen eating Billy's head on the plate, poked his head around the door and even in the darkened room, the whites of the maniac's eyes seemed almost to fluoresce. He smiled, and ran the tip of his tongue around his lips.

'Uncle Alf!' Barry screamed at the top of his voice, 'Help! Murder! Murder!'

The man who the late Billy had referred to as Mr Wroot, gritted his teeth at the yelling boy and gave a threatening cut-throat gesture by drawing his index finger-tip across his fat Adam's apple.

All of a sudden, Davy hurled the vase at Wroot and it smashed squarely in his face, and the fragments of the vase scattered everywhere. Wroot let out a loud grunt, and blood blossomed from a large cut on his forehead, just over his right eyebrow. He lunged across the room at the boys, and Barry dived on to the floor and scrambled under the bed, and a second later, Davy did the same. They then bolted like rats from under the bed and ran to the doorway with Wroot a few feet behind them. The boys ran downstairs and across the hall and tried to get out via the front door, but the old rusty bolt on the bottom of the door wouldn't budge. Davy slammed the vestibule door behind him and sandwiched between that door and the front door, he and Barry tried to yank back the bolt. Davy looked at the frosted glass of the vestibule door, expecting to see Wroot's evil face peer through it at any moment.

'Help us open it, come on!' Barry groaned, putting all his might into shifting the damned bolt.

There came a steady thump on the carpeted stairs.

'He's coming!' cried Davy, and he tried with every ounce of his strength to pull that bolt back, and it seemed to be slowly moving.

Barry looked back at the vestibule door and saw a shadow on the pale glass pane. That door opened.

Both boys cried out, horrified at what was about to happen.

But thankfully it was only Alf, and although he was furious at the screams, he had obviously seen Wroot's blood from the injury he had sustained from the vase. 'Who's hurt himself?' he said, and he reached for the light switch and clicked it on.

The boys gave their account of the cannibal at large in the house and when Davy said, 'The man who gave you a fat lip is a cannibal, Alf,' Alf became enraged and said to him, 'You will never, and I mean, never, set foot in here again! Pack your things right now, you little runt!' This violent reaction to Davy's comments was incomprehensible to the lads.

And that morning, despite Aggie's loud and colourful protestations, Alf marched the boys to the house of a neighbour who had a car, and got him to drive the boys to their homes in Bootle.

Barry's parents simply couldn't believe the far-fetched story of secret passages in Aggie's house and the cannibal who ate the little boy. Davy's parents just laughed and said he had a very vivid imagination when he gave his account of the strange and terrifying goings-on at the house on Cambridge Street, and gradually, over the years, the boys drifted apart, and whenever they told anyone about it, their accounts were met with scepticism, and who could really blame anyone for disbelieving such a incredible and fanciful story?

A few years ago, Barry, now a father of four in his forties, wrote to me to tell me about the extraordinary incidents from all those years ago, and he and I tracked down Davy, who was working in a call centre in Kent. Barry wasn't very computer savant, and never even bothered with email, and he wasn't aware that Davy had a Facebook page. When we caught up with Davy, he confirmed the story and the two men now stay in touch. I talked to a psychologist, and he told me that he knows of many people who suddenly recall very bizarre incidents from their childhood which they often dismiss as a faulty memory or a memory of a dream which has been filed away as a real occurrence. I talked about this case briefly on a radio programme and did not mention Cambridge Street, and a woman later contacted me with a strange story which seemed to add some credence to Barry and Davy's frightening experiences. Tina, a woman in her fifties, who lived on Crown Street, Edge Hill, in the 1970s, said she used to be friends with a girl named Maureen who lived on Cambridge Street in the early 1970s, and she had heard the story of the secret passages under houses on Cambridge Street and once heard Maureen's grandmother talk about 'a dirty old man' named Wroot who was a well-known landlord of several houses in the area around Cambridge Street. Wroot – and Maureen's grandmother would always emphasise the silent 'W' at the beginning of the man's surname, was said to lurk in the cellars of his house and stand under the ventilation grids so he could look up women's skirts. The other depraved things this man got up to could not be put into print in a book such as this or I would risk prosecution under the Obscene Publications Act. I asked Tina if Maureen's grandmother ever mentioned Wroot playing a piano, but Tina said she couldn't recall that he did. The period when this man was carrying out his disgusting activities would probably be around Edwardian times, and this leads me to believe that Barry and Davy, and Uncle Alf, must have been dealing with ghosts, so this makes me to wonder if the secret passages were also ethereal, or whether a timeslip situation was the cause of the nightmarish phenomena.

BURIED ALIVE

One unusually sunny Sunday afternoon in the October of 1892, a middle-aged joiner named Bill Eckersley left his house at 51 Chester Road in Tuebrook and headed for nearby Newsham Park, where he liked to walk on Sundays after his usual roast dinner. On this afternoon, he saw a rather sinister-looking black four-wheeled carriage, known as a 'growler' coming along West Derby Road from the east. Eckersley waited for the carriage to pass, but instead it pulled up at the kerb six feet in front of him and two tall men in bowler hats alighted from it and hurried towards the joiner, who was startled by their quick approach.

'Mr Eckersley, sir,' said one of the tall pair. He seemed to be about thirty and sported a large black walrus moustache. Before the carpenter could utter a word the men came to each side of him and seized him by his arms. Eckersley was bundled into the carriage where a third man pointed a pistol at the joiner. The man with the walrus moustache then produced a bag made of some dark canvas-like material and put it over Eckersley's head. The joiner sat there in an understandably terrified state, and he felt the carriage swerve around and go back the way it had arrived. 'What's the meaning of this?' Eckersley asked, trembling as he thought of the gun pointed at him. Why was he being abducted? He hoped that it was perhaps some jest, but as the growler trundled on for a long time that was very difficult to gauge, Eckersley thought he would never see his wife and children again. At one point in the journey, the joiner heard the peel of church bells, and some time after that he heard the distinctive sound of an Italian street musician's barrel organ, and whenever he asked where he was being taken, he'd feel the barrel of the gun jabbed between his ribs.

At last the growler came to a halt and Eckersley was guided out of the carriage and taken into a house with an echoing hallway. He was taken down a flight of stone steps which felt hard and cold beneath his shoes, and here the bag was removed from his head. Billy Eckersley found himself in a cellar workshop illuminated by six oil lamps. Here and there were stacks of quality wood and carpentry tools of every sort, and the centre of the cellar was dominated by a large workbench equipped with several vices.

The man with the walrus moustache unfurled a long roll of paper on the desk and placed boxes of tacks and nails at each corner of the sheet to prevent it from curling up. Eckersley could see that this paper featured the blueprint of a very strange item indeed – an unusually broad coffin that was almost heart-shaped. 'We have a friend who would like you to make this as soon as possible,' walrus moustache said in a well-spoken accentless voice, and he tapped the index finger of his black leather-gloved hand on the unusual design.

'Why have I been brought here? What's going on?' Billy Eckersley demanded to know.

'You were brought here to make this coffin,' said walrus moustache. 'That's what's going on. The sooner you make this the sooner we will return you to your home.'

'Why couldn't you have just asked me to make it, instead of resorting to kidnapping me?' asked the carpenter.

The second abductor, who also wore a bowler hat, said to the carpenter: 'You're not in any position to question what we say, Mr Eckersley. Now, you must do what we say or meet your fate.'

Billy Eckersley reluctantly worked around the clock sawing the wood and skilfully fitting together the bizarrely-shaped coffin, and after eight hours, he was given a meal and a glass of beer. And then he resumed his work, and when he had finished the job, a few hours after the break, he asked the two men if they required the coffin to be varnished, and they said they didn't. They inspected the coffin, which measured a little over six feet in length and four and a half feet in width, and both agreed that Eckersley had done an excellent job. The man with the heavy moustache took the bag from his pocket, ready to put it on the joiner's head for the return journey, when the door to the cellar burst open, and in ran a young barefooted woman of about twenty to twenty-five years of age, dressed in a long white nightgown. She had dark circles around her bulging mad-looking eyes, and she threw her arms out to Eckersley and tried to run to him but the two abductors intercepted her and began to drag her out of the room.

'Help me!' she screamed, 'They're going to bury me alive!'

Eckersley shook with fear when he heard this, and felt so helpless as he watched the two men drag the poor young woman out of the cellar. Her small white hands made a desperate attempt to grasp at the architrave of the door but they peeled her fingers from the doorframe and shouted profanities at her. Then came the sound of a door being slammed and locked, and the two men returned to take the joiner back to his neighbourhood – or would they perhaps shoot him and dump his body in some remote spot, thereby insuring that their dastardly intentions would never be discovered?

Billy Eckersley sweated copiously under his hood during the return journey, for he expected to receive a bullethole in his skull at any moment. But at last the growler came to a halt on Snaefell Avenue, off West Derby Road. It was night-time, and there was a torrential downpour. Eckersley was thrown out of the carriage with the bag still on his head, and almost immediately, the growler tore off into the night. The carpenter ripped the bag off his head and looked for the carriage but it was gone, although he thought he could hear it rattling round the corner of Sutton Street, headed for the Green Lane thoroughfare. Eckersley went home, where his frantic wife and children were so relieved to see him. He told his wife what had happened and she urged him to go to the police – which he did – later that night. The police sergeant Eckersley talked to was very sceptical about the story, and said there was little he could do when he had so little information to go on. Eckersley told him he recalled the peel of a church bells and the sounds of an Italian street musician's barrel organ during the journey, but the sergeant just shook his head and said all that was too vague to serve as a clue. Billy Eckersley left the police station in Tuebrook feeling bitter, and disillusioned, but then came a surprising development. A local coachman named David Rees was going up West Derby Road a week after the abduction and pulled up his carriage when he saw Eckersley to tell him that he had witnessed him being abducted on the previous Sunday. Rees said he had tried to follow the growler, but had lost it near Deysbrook Lane when a hansom cab collided with the coach he was driving. Rees had seen the mysterious black growler several times since and felt it was connected to Croxteth Hall – which lay in the general direction it was headed that Sunday.

When Eckersley told the coachman about the special coffin he was forced to build and the claims of the woman in the white gown, Rees vowed to track down the abductors, but found his quest thwarted by the police who, seemed to warn him off from delving into the strange goings-on. And both Eckersley and Rees were visited in the dead of night by shadowy men who warned them to stop prying into matters that did not concern them.

Around this time there were rumours circulating that a woman had been buried alive next to the body of her wealthy lover in a special coffin in a grave in Anfield cemetery. The burial had taken place at three in the morning. The bizarre ritual was said to have been carried out by disciples of the dead man, an aristocrat who had worshipped the Devil. The thought of the young woman who had begged for help from Billy Eckersley, being buried alongside the corpse of her lover, haunted the joiner for many years.

The earth beneath our feet holds many such macabre secrets, and this has been just one of them.

THE WHITE DOT

There are certain things, certain phenomena, reported to me regularly by the readers of my books and columns, which I have a hard time explaining, and the following story belongs to this class of inexplicable mystery.

One rainy evening in the October of 1963, a woman in her mid-thirties named Rita, was recovering from a bout of the flu, and she sat in her armchair, which had been dragged close to the two-bar electric fire with her hands cupped around a mug of cocoa as she watched an episode of the popular western series *Bonanza* on her little 16-inch black and white television set. Perhaps I should point out at this point that Rita's husband was working nights at a factory, and had set off to work around 8pm, and would not be expected back home until around six in the morning. The couple's two children, Tina, aged 13, and Susan who had just turned 15, were staying with Rita's sister Ann, over on Leyfield Road, West Derby. Rita's home was situated on Melwood Drive, and she and her family had lived there for almost five years. Rita was not a woman who entertained the thought of anything supernatural, nor could she acknowledge the existence of ghosts. She was a down-to-earth housewife, and so, when the strange incidents which I am about to document took place, Rita was left shocked and unnerved by the experiences.

After *Bonanza* had finished at around 8.55pm, Rita got up from her armchair, gripped the large silvered tuning wheel and turned it away from the Granada channel towards BBC1, just in time to catch the last few minutes of the medical drama series *Doctor Finlay's Casebook*. After that came the news, and then *The Dick Van Dyke Show*, which Rita was fond of, but the flu was making her feel drowsy, and about half way through the American comedy show, she fell asleep, and when she awoke, *The Dick Van Dyke Show* had ended and a boring piano recital was being shown, so Rita turned the tuner back to Granada, and watched the programmes there for a while, but again dozed off. She woke again at around 11.50, and then a few minutes later, the television stations closed down. Remote control consoles were very rare in those days, and so, Rita got up and switched off the television, then, feeling too drained to get up, she sat for a moment and saw the white dot appear. This dot is never seen today because of the advanced screens we have in modern our television sets, but in the 1960s, when a set was switched off, the picture on screen would collapse and shrink to a bright luminous dot a bit smaller than a decimal penny. This came about as the capacitors (which store power in the set) discharged and the cathode-ray tube would continue to emit electrons without the beam being moved horizontally or vertically. People often joked about being so addicted to television that they watched it all day until the white dot appeared at night when the stations closed down.

Well on this night, Rita happened to look at the little luminous dot, which normally faded after about 15 seconds, but on this occasion, the dot persisted and did not change for about a minute, and Rita felt as if there was something almost hypnotic about the glowing point. It began to expand, and as it did so a face appeared within it – a grinning face set in a head – a bald head. Rita was more stunned than scared, and she looked away for a moment, squeezed her eyes shut, thinking the flu was making her see things that weren't there. She looked back at the screen, and the grinning face was still there, and seemed even more sharply defined now. As she looked on, she saw that the tiny mouth of the luminous face was opening and closing as if words were being spoken, and suddenly, as clear as a bell, she heard a voice which sounded as if it was far off, and this voice was calling to her.

'Rita ... Rita ...'

Frightened and confused, she stood up and left the living room to go into the hall. Should she call on her neighbour June, who lived next door, and tell her what she had just seen and heard, or should she stay put? A quick peep into the living room revealed that the luminous dot had now faded away, so she hurried into the room and unplugged the television, then went up to bed, where she thought of the strange incident for a while until she drifted off into an uncomfortable sleep because of her flu.

At 6.20am, Rita's husband Hugh came home, and when he got into bed, she told him what had happened, and predictably, he said she'd seen the face in the dot and heard her name being called because she'd probably had a temperature because of her illness. Hugh was soon snoring, and Rita got up soon afterwards. Despite having no appetite, she tried to eat a bowl of cornflakes, and then she went into the living room and looked at the television set in the cold light of morning. Hugh was probably right, she had probably been seeing and hearing things – or at least she hoped she had.

That evening at 8pm, Hugh set off for the factory night shift, and once again the girls stayed over at their aunt's house on Leyfield Road. Rita's flu seemed to have lifted somewhat, and she sat there drinking tea and enjoying a Turkish Delight her husband had bought her as she watched the television. She enjoyed a film which started around 8.10pm, and then smoked a few cigarettes as she enjoyed *Comedy Playhouse*. During the news at 10pm, Rita browsed the *Liverpool Echo*, and then around half-past ten she watched one of her favourite shows on the box – *That Was The Week That Was*, a satirical programme presented by David Frost. The show ended around a 11.15, and not long afterwards the television channels closed down for the night. Rita turned the off button and once again the white dot appeared in the centre of the screen – and it quickly transformed itself into that grinning, impish face.

'Oh God!' Rita gasped.

'Rita ... Rita ...' came the voice in the distance. This time Rita could gauge just exactly where the voice coming from – the direction of the television set.

She suddenly found herself unable to move, and she fell into what she could only describe as a dream-like state, rather like the state of consciousness the mind shifts into between waking and sleeping. The luminous bald head on the screen expanded as it went out of focus, and a circle opened up with images within it, and those images were very spooky indeed. Two silhouettes of men sitting at a desk in a huge luxurious office swam into view, and in American accents, they chatted to one another. One man said to the other: 'He wants us to join up with the commies and we can't do that. We can never do that.'

And then that scene dissolved, and Rita saw a man in an open-topped car moving along through what looked like a pleasant green park. Somehow, Rita knew what was about to happen. One of the men she had seen in the office was lying in some sort of underground den, and he was aiming an unusually long rifle at the man in the car. The barrel of the rifle was protruding from a flower-bed in a garden to the left of the man in the car, who had a woman beside him – possibly his wife. Rita heard the loud, ear-piercing crack from the rifle after a number of other gunshot sounds had echoed through the living room. What came next was truly horrific. The head of the man in the car exploded as the bullet from the rifle hit him from behind and just to his left. The front of the head flew open and a cloud of blood and atomised brain matter billowed into the sunlight.

Rita suddenly regained the power to move, and she let out a scream, and then she ran out of the living room and stayed in the kitchen for a while, where she trembled as she digested the significance of what she had just witnessed. Was she going mad? It couldn't be the flu as her appetite had returned and she had felt a lot better than the day before. Rita didn't dare tell her husband because he would definitely think she was going insane.

A month later, Rita, like millions across the world, was shocked and saddened to learn of the mysterious murder of US President John Fitzgerald Kennedy at Dallas on 22 November. Only then did Rita recognise who the man had been in that 'vision' which was seemingly induced by the white dot on the television – it had been the head of JFK she had seen exploding. But the press and television reports made no mention of a violent explosion of blood from the President's head – most people who watched the television reports and read the newspaper articles had the impression that the bullets had merely entered the President's back and head and killed him.

Many years later, the controversial footage of the actual assassination of Kennedy, is routinely viewed by members of the public via YouTube, and this footage – shot by Abraham Zapruder on a Bell & Howell 8mm cine camera, and therefore known as the Zapruder Film – clearly, and graphically, shows the front of Kennedy's head explode as a high-velocity bullet seems to enter from behind and to the left. This bullet then leaves the President's head from the front-right area, leaving a ghastly flap of skin and other tissue dangling from the exit wound. This is exactly what Rita saw that October night, a month before the assassination took place. The official verdict is that Lee Harvey Oswald single-handedly shot the President with a rifle from the window of a nearby building, but the angle of the exit wound in the final head shot to Kennedy suggests that the assassin was to the left and behind the President – almost diagonally opposite the 'Grassy Knoll' area so favoured by conspiracy theorists – but is there any evidence to back up the presence of a gunman in that location?

The House Select Committee of Assassinations – the official investigating body assigned to the assassination – concluded that Oswald was solely responsible, but a great deal of evidence suggests otherwise, including the alleged accidental recording of the gunshots by a police motorcyclist's dictabelt recorder. The recordings came from a motorcycle police officer who was travelling about 200 feet behind the President's car, and puts the source of the gunshots to the left and back of Kennedy. A very mysterious woman was also standing close to this area as Kennedy was shot, and she has never been identified, but is nicknamed the 'Babushka Lady', because she resembles a traditional Russian grandmother in her attire – a dowdy-looking mac and headscarf which is tied under her chin. This individual, who seems to be using a cine camera, is apparently filming the assassination of Kennedy from much closer quarters than Abraham Zapruder, who captured her in his own film for a second or so. The whole assassination has spawned countless books, movies and documentaries, and a recent poll in the United States has shown that most Americans believe that President Kennedy was not killed by Lee Harvey Oswald, but hired hitmen (who were possibly military-trained) for some political reason. The truth behind the assassination will be revealed in time to come, when most of the conspirators are dead, but in the meantime, theories abound as to why the 35th President of the United States was murdered in Dallas on that eventful Friday in November 1963. In Rita's strange vision, she said she had clearly seen two silhouetted Americans, and one of them had said to the other: 'He wants us to join up with the commies and we can't do that. We can never do that.'

The idea of Kennedy wanting the Russians to join up with the Americans may seem ludicrous, but there is a little-known fact concerning JFK that may tie in with this paranormal mystery and even throw some light on the Dallas assassination. In October 1963, shortly before Rita had her weird premonition, which was seen in the white dot of the TV screen, President Kennedy came out with a curious proposal which he put to the Soviet Premiere Nikita S. Khrushchev: he asked the Russians if they would be willing to join forces with the US to explore the Moon. The strongly-worded proposal of a joint American-Russian manned lunar programme was put forward by Kennedy in a speech before the United Nations General Assembly on 20 September 1963, in New York. Many right-wingers in the US Senate were horrified when Kennedy stated that joint missions to the Moon with Russians and American astronauts working together 'would require a new approach to the Cold War'. Many of those right-wingers breathed a sigh of relief when Kruschev's government rejected Kennedy's proposal – but then, unknown to most of us in the West at that time, Kruschev told his closest comrades in private that perhaps the USSR should accept Kennedy's offer – but weeks later, the US President was murdered in very sinister circumstances, and of course, the person who was widely publicised as the assassin – Lee Harvey Oswald – was himself murdered before he could even stand trial. Had the Soviet Union teamed up with the United States, a lot of armament dealers and manufacturers of Cold War missiles would have undoubtedly lost billions of dollars.

After Rita recovered from her flu, she never again saw anything strange in her television screen, but for some time, whenever she switched off her television set, she would deliberately avoid looking at that white dot.

THE PHANTOM MONKS OF CHILDWALL

At a little ad hoc book signing after a talk on ghosts in October 2011, an obsessive man who has stalked me for many years approached with his head bowed and slid a copy of my *Haunted City* on the table for me to sign for his daughter. This man is often found on a certain well-known Liverpool forum, where he constantly criticises me and accuses me of all kinds of skulduggery. Not only has he visited places where I have been living, he also once visited a friend's street under the pretence of being lost, just to see if he could catch a glimpse of me there. Whenever I am at a public event, be it an appearance at the history fair at St George's Hall or a talk I am giving somewhere, you can guarantee that the stalker will be waiting there in the shadows with his mobile phone, waiting to take a sneak picture (which he then publishes on the forum he frequents). I don't mind him taking pictures of me, as that's perfectly legal in a public place, but if there is a niece or nephew present, or some other minor who is related to me, or the little boy or girl of someone getting their book signed in the shot, I take objection to people of the stalker's sick mentality capturing these innocent children on video or in stills. The stalker is so out of touch with reality, he doesn't realise that some fellow members of his forum love winding him up by deliberately mentioning me, just to get him to post a rant, and he falls for it every time. On the following occasion he and a fellow nut from the same forum came to a book signing, and while his friend videoed me on his phone, the stalker tried to catch me out so he'd have material for his beloved forum life. I know this because someone who frequents the forum of obsessives told me. The stalker said, 'Hey Tom, there are a lot of ghosts knocking about aren't there? How can you write all these books when there must be a limited amount of ghosts, like?'

I addressed him by his first name to give him a little shock, because any psychologist will tell you that the stalker who thinks he hasn't been sussed by his prey recoils in horror when he discovers they know his name. I told him that two days back, the United Nations had announced that the world's population had reached seven billion, and I also informed him that whilst this figure is alarmingly high, the dead still outnumber the living. For every living person there are fifteen dead ones, with 107 billion dead since written records began. The official figure for the number of people who have lived, if you are interested, is 107,602,707,791 (and obviously this figure will have gone up since the statistics were published by the Population Reference Bureau, and will have risen by thousands by the time you reach the end of this book). So, if many ghosts are images – be they sentient or as conscious as a television picture – then we shouldn't be too surprised there are a lot of them about when we see that the dead still outnumber us by fifteen to one. The stalker and his pocket cameraman fled when they realised they had received a good answer to the question about 'a lot of ghosts knocking about'.

Well, even stalkers can pose some interesting questions, and there certainly are a lot of ghosts 'knocking about' – not just in Liverpool, but particularly in Britain; in fact the *Guinness Book of Records* stated, some years ago, that Britain has more ghosts per square mile than many other countries, and this is due, no doubt, to our long and bloody history. Some ghosts are rarely noticed as they walk among us because they are the carnate manifestations of people who have recently died, and so their clothing, being fairly modern, does not seem out of the ordinary, but Victorian ghosts – men with their top hats and women with their long black dresses (often crinoline ones) are immediately noticed if they appear amongst modern folk. Regency period ghosts in white periwigs have been seen around Liverpool, and several medieval-looking ones as well, and these latter types are the subject of the following story, related to me many years ago by Louise from Childwall.

In 1995, 29-year-old Louise and her 39-year-old husband Duncan were elated to move out of their crumbling damp house in Kensington into a lovely semi-detached house in Childwall. Duncan had received compensation from a serious accident at his workplace the year before, and Louise's auntie had died, leaving her a lot of money in the will, and so the couple decided to go house-hunting, and Louise found the house of her dreams in Childwall, just a stone's throw from the Childwall Abbey pub. The couple moved into the house in the summer of 1995, and Duncan got a job working nights at a factory near Haydock, and although Louise was not happy sleeping alone at nights, Duncan assured her he would have a word with the boss at his works soon to see if he could get on to the day shift, and if the boss said that wasn't possible, Duncan would find another job where he could work days.

It was a humid July night when Louise first slept alone at the new house. She felt fine, even though she was on her own. She sat reading a teenage magazine called *Sugar* which her young sister Jenny had left during her visit in the afternoon, and Louise found the teen magazine rather amusing; full of personality tests, advice on first-time sex and so on. It was around one in the morning when Louise finally dropped off, and although Duncan had advised her not to, she had left the window open a few inches. Who would be able to get up to an upstairs window, Louise had reasoned, and she preferred the night-time breeze filtering into the stuffy room rather than an electric

43

fan which had started to make an irritating clicking sound as it swept left and right. Around 2.20am, something woke her; she wasn't sure if it was a noise inside the room, or somewhere outside in the suburban Childwall night, but she looked around the room and most of the light shining into the bedroom was from the moon, which was full that night. There was also a faint glow from a bluish mercury-vapour lamp from the street, about a hundred yards distant.

Louise turned over and her left hand pounded the pillow to soften it up a bit. She tried to relax and drive out thoughts about being alone, and away from Duncan, when she suddenly heard some sort of music in the distance. She opened her eyes and listened. It sounded like monks chanting. Immediately, Louise thought someone had a radio or a CD player on in the distance, and the music sounded just like *Enigma* – the musical project founded by Michael Cretu, David Fairstein and Frank Peterson. *Enigma* was storming the charts around that time and the music used Gregorian chants to give the hits a monastic feel. Louise, however, was something of a music fan, and when she concentrated hard on the distant chanting she became quite sure that the sound they were producing was not like any *Enigma* CD she had heard, and she found the deep liturgical voices quite unsettling.

The chanting seemed to fade away after a few minutes, and Louise convinced herself that she had merely heard the audio to some film on a television somewhere, and she fell asleep.

She was rudely awakened around 3am by someone with an ice-cold hand grabbing at her right wrist as she lay on her back in bed. Louise's eyelids flew open when she realised there was someone there, and to her utter horror, she saw two figures wearing the attire of hooded monks, standing at the bottom of her bed. The cowls they wore were of a darkish brown material, and she could hardly see the faces of the monks in their pointed hoods. One of these eerie bedroom visitors said something in a rich deep voice, and the words sounded as if they were in Latin. The only one of these words that Louise could make out was 'Albion' – which is an archaic name for Britain (in fact it's the oldest known name for Britain). Louise screamed at the intruders, who had been standing side by side, but now they parted – and one went round the left side of the bed and the other came round the right hand side. The face of the one on the right could now be partially seen as the faint lamplight outside caught the right side of his face. This 'monk' was a smooth-featured man with pallid skin who seemed to be about thirty. Louise's screams did not provoke the least reaction in the hooded prowlers, and simultaneously they bent over her and one of them clamped an icy hand over her mouth and grabbed her forearm to drag her towards the bottom of the bed as the other monk seized her other arm and dragged her in a likewise fashion.

Louise was wearing nothing on this humid night, and as her stomach slid across the cold brass piping at the end of the bed, she began to cry, thinking she might be raped or perhaps murdered by the two men who were obviously unbalanced to be dressing up as monks. At this point, Louise noticed that the wall facing the bed, towards which she was being dragged, was not there any more. In its place was a dark passageway of some sort, and Louise seems to have a faint recollection of sandstone carvings along the walls and cold wide stony steps. At the end of this passageway, she could make out a cluster of candles burning on a tall stand. She also recalled detecting a sweet scent which reminded her of church incense. Louise passed out as she entered the passageway, and vaguely recalls being carried by the hooded men.

She woke up screaming on her bed at around five in the morning with the blankets and pillow in disarray. By the welcome light of that summer morning, Louise saw that her heavy mahogany chest of drawers, which had stood against the right wall – as seen from the bed – had been dragged a few feet away towards the door, and the middle drawer was open. Louise got up, threw on some underwear and a nightie, and went downstairs to smoke numerous cigarettes in the kitchen as she tried to fathom out what had happened. She rooted through the drawer in the kitchen trying to find the work number her husband had left her, but was unable to find the scrap of paper anywhere. She realised he would be back at 7am anyway, but how on earth could she expect him to believe what had taken place earlier in the morning? So she did not tell him what had happened immediately, and when she did he knew his wife was not lying from the look of fear in her eyes. Duncan believed the house was haunted and said that they should perhaps start looking for somewhere else, but Louise shook her head and said, 'No, we're staying put. I think if I saw those figures again I'd kill them. No one's making us leave here, not even ghosts.'

'How can you kill them if they're already dead?' joked Duncan nervously, and he asked to have a look at his wife's body to see if the intruders were flesh and blood characters who had perhaps belonged to some cult. 'If they've touched you in any way, I'll bleedin' kill them myself, never mind you killin' them!' Duncan said through clenched teeth. There wasn't a mark on Louise's body, and Duncan said he'd have to pack in his job rather than have his wife go through another weird episode at the house. Louise said she'd bring her younger sister Jenny over, but Duncan was angry at the suggestion. 'And what's a young girl going to do if those things do come back? I'll find a decent daytime job, love. Don't you worry.'

But as the day developed into a hot and sunny affair, Louise convinced her husband that the whole thing with the monks had been some lucid dream. 'Yeah, but what about the chest of drawers? Something pulled them out,' Duncan reasoned.

'Well, sleepwalkers move things about,' retorted Louise, 'it's well known. My cousin used to leave his bed at all hours in the morning and sleepwalk around starkers adjusting the paintings in his lounge.'

Duncan finally got some sleep and reluctantly agreed to go to work at 8pm. By then, seventeen-year-old Jenny had arrived, and of course, her big sister Louise never said anything about the monks.

Jenny watched MTV and sat talking about boys and Take That and which Spice Girl she looked like. She also had a voracious appetite for such a slim girl and she ate her way through every Magnum ice cream in the freezer and even demolished the remainder of Duncan's birthday cake. At one in the morning, Jenny admitted that she had started smoking cigarettes and asked Louise if she could have one of hers. Louise said, 'No, they're bad for your health, Jenny; you're not smoking.' Louise then muted the television because Jenny had switched over to The Box channel and had the volume on full.

'Oh go on, don't be such an old spoil sport – pretty please, Louise,' the girl begged, and Louise saw the funny side of the unintentional rhyme of 'please Louise' and relented, saying, 'Okay ... just this once ... and I mean it, no more after this.'

Jenny lit the cigarette and kept giggling because Louise was watching her. 'It's mad, you watching me, oh I feel terrible smoking in front of you,' the girl said, blushing.

All of a sudden in the silence (because of the muted television) both young women heard faint chanting somewhere. 'What's the hell's that?' Jenny asked her sister, reading the concern on Louise's face. Louise was quite scared, and she went into the hallway and checked that the security chain had been put on the front door. 'Louise, what's up? You're scaring me,' said Jenny, following closely behind her sister as she went to the kitchen to get a huge carving knife from the cutlery drawer.

'Nothing, it's okay, Jen,' Louise said, and her trembling hand took the knife from the drawer and placed it on the draining board.

'Louise what's going on?' Jenny raised her voice and coughed as she accidentally inhaled the cigarette smoke too far back into her lungs.

There were thuds upstairs.

Both girls looked up at the kitchen ceiling.

Jenny yelped, 'Who's that? Did you just hear what I heard?'

Then came a thump on the hallway ceiling – which meant someone was coming along the landing upstairs. By now, the sounds of monks chanting – that very same chanting Louise had heard the night before – could clearly be heard in the rooms upstairs.

'Come on, Jenny!' bawled Louise, and she picked up the knife with one hand and with the other hand she dragged Jenny to the front door and began to unfasten the chain.

Both sisters saw male sandalled feet appear on the top step of the stairs, and Jenny screamed. Louise opened the door and the two of

47

them hurried out into the cool summer night. Louise looked up at her bedroom window and saw that something was glowing in the room and casting shadows against the lace curtains – it looked like a procession of monks in their cowls moving from right to left.

The sisters ran off down the street, and bumped into an elderly man, a Mr Serridge, who was out walking his dog because of a bout of insomnia. Mr Serridge, seeing the large knife in Louise's hand, thought he was about to be mugged, and knew his little Jack Russell would not be of any use to repel his imagined mugger, so he was greatly relieved when he learnt that the girls were fleeing from something and not about to attack him. When Mr Serridge heard Louise mention monks, the word seemed to strike some chord in the elderly dog-walker, and he inhaled sharply then said, 'Oh, so they're back then, are they?' And he looked in the direction of Louise's house, which was just visible through the trees.

'You know about them?' Louise asked, hoping the old man could somehow help her or at least cast some light on what was going on. What he said in reply only served to jangle the nerves of the two sisters.

As far back as he could remember, said Serridge, there had been stories about Devil-worshipping monks who emerged from some subterranean abbey that lay somewhere beneath the ground close to that mysterious stretch of land known as 'Bloody Acre'. This traditionally accursed field, which runs alongside the graveyard of All Saints Church, has been known as Bloody Acre since time immemorial, and no one – not one historian – has ever found out why, but many supposedly learned local historians have claimed that the field obtained its sanguineous title because of some mere unreported skirmish in the English Civil War – but long before the days of Cromwell, that field was said to be a place to avoid and respect. All sorts of things have been seen and heard over, on and beneath Bloody Acre – phantom explosions, strange subterranean bells and weird incantations, and some have even claimed to have seen the emergence of a huge black vaporous Angel of Death who shows himself before a major war on the Acre.

As the old man talked about Bloody Acre, Jenny bent down and stroked his Jack Russell, and she smiled as the dog rolled on to his back with his head back so she could tickle him under his chin. Then all of a sudden the dog let out a loud yelp, which startled the girls, and then it craned its neck and pulled on its leash as it stared at something further down the suburban drive. It was one of those monks, silhouetted by the feeble lamp post shining behind him. 'Oh my God! Oh no!' shrieked Louise, and Jenny cowered behind her.

'Don't be afraid,' said Mr Serridge, and then to Louise, 'Hold him a minute,' and he handed the dog's lead to her. The old man then walked towards the monk, and the figure stopped in its tracks.

'Mr Serridge halted about six feet away from the figure and spat on the ground between himself and the baleful-looking entity. 'In the name of the Lord, what do you wish?' Mr Serridge shouted to the apparition, and as Louise and Jenny, and the little frightened dog looked on, the monk instantly vanished. Mr Serridge then walked back to the trembling sisters and said, 'Stay at my house until morning if you want. Someone must have conjured them up again.'

Louise was speechless for a while, and then she said, 'We can't, we've left the front door open.'

'I'll go and shut it, what number is it?' said the brave old man.

'I haven't got the keys or anything ... oh I just don't know what to do,' replied Louise, and then she added, 'Are you sure we can stay in yours?'

'Yes,' said Mr Serridge, 'I'm a widower, and I live on my own.'

'My husband will be back around seven,' Louise recalled, and Mr Serridge nodded and said, 'Well you'll be okay in my place till then. Are you sure you haven't left the fire on or anything?'

Louise hugged Jenny, who seemed very afraid, and said: 'No, there's nothing switched on. Thanks very much.'

And the elderly man went off as his dog let out a yelp and tilted its head as it watched its master walk away. Serridge returned about three minutes later and said, 'Hope you don't mind, but I went in the house and found your keys, just in case you want to go home.'

'Ah, thanks,' Louise said, 'what's your name? My name's Louise and this is my sister Jenny.'

'Jacob,' Mr Serridge answered. 'Call me Jake if you want.'

Serridge looked after the sisters until 7am. He gave Jenny glass after glass of Vimto and every flavour of crisp, bag after bag. He told Louise that someone in the area was known to dabble in witchcraft 'and that sort of stuff' and this irresponsible person had caused these monks to walk before. Serridge hinted that this person – who he would not name – might have even targeted Louise because she was a newcomer. 'They're a real clique round here,' Serridge said with a dismissive shake of his head, 'well some of them anyway.'

'Well I think I'll be moving,' said Louise, admitting defeat at last. 'I couldn't put up with another night like this.'

'You've got a really bad rash on the back of your neck, Louise,' Jenny noted, and pulled back the flimsy collar of her sister's nightgown to get a better look at it. 'I always get that with nerves,' said Louise.

Serridge said he would make a number of crosses out of rowan branches later in the morning and bind them with red thread, and he explained that such crosses had always been used as 'ghost repellents'. Louise told him not to bother, but later that day, Mr Serridge came to her home while her husband was fast asleep in bed, and gave her six of the crosses. He told her to put one in each room. He would also ask a local nun he knew to say prayers to protect the house. That night, Louise pretended she was going to stay at her mother's house, and went over to Huyton to have her tea with her, but when Duncan was at work, she got a taxi back to the house. Now that she had a friend in the neighbourhood she decided that if anything supernatural took place, she would leave immediately and stay at Mr Serridge's home, but that night, nothing remotely paranormal took place, and Louise and Duncan stayed at the house, where they still live happily today.

TIME OUT OF JOINT

The following story fascinates me for two reasons. Firstly, it hints that our existence is but one version of reality, and that many worlds similar to our own exist next to one another in layers, rather like the pages of a very thick book. I also find this story fascinating because I am referenced in it, and that is rather rare in these stories.

In the winter of 2009, a twenty-one-year-old Indian-born student named Indra, who was studying economics and sociology at Liverpool University, began to suffer from intense headaches. Indra's friends constantly advised him to go and see his doctor, but the student had always had a long-standing phobia of being diagnosed with various terminal conditions, and was well-known as the hypochondriac of his family. He decided to bury his head in the sand with regard to his headaches and tried his best to carry on with his studies by taking paracetamol every four hours. This regime of self-medication went on for weeks with no lessening of his symptoms. Then Indra started to take Co-Drydamol, progressing eventually to even stronger analgesics. The headaches became more severe, and during one particularly bad headache in the library at the university, Indra began to sniffle, and fresh bright red oxygenated blood dripped from his nose and blotted the pages of the book he was reading. The student almost hyperventilated with shock when he saw the blood, because he was convinced that such nosebleeds accompanied with such crippling headaches were a sure sign of an aggressive brain tumour.

Indra left the library and went to the toilet, where he mopped his nose with tissue and held back his head as he panted with anxiety in one of the cubicles. Once he was sure the nosebleed had stopped, he left the library and walked aimlessly among the crowds in the city centre of Liverpool, convinced he was dying. Indra was walking up Ranelagh Street, and passing a shop called Dawsons, which sold musical instruments, when he spotted a former college friend named Craig coming out of the shop in his wheelchair, which was being pushed by his girlfriend, Jaclyn. Indra didn't want to talk to Craig at that moment, because he felt so down regarding his 'terminal' condition, and so he crossed the road and nipped down Fairclough Street, which leads on to Lawton and Cropper Streets – back streets behind the former Lewis's building. Indra thought he heard Craig shout after him as he crossed Ranelagh Street but he did not turn round.

As Indra was walking from the back street towards Newington, which leads on to Renshaw Street, he had a 'funny turn'. He felt dizzy, out of breath, and also experienced a weird tingling sensation in his head. The sensation passed after less than a minute, and Indra was now convinced he was seriously ill, and when he reached Renshaw Street, his heart was palpitating and his mouth was bone dry. He went to a newsagents to get a bottle of water, and it was here, in the midst of his hyper-anxiety, that he noticed something odd. On the front of all of the tabloid newspapers, there were headlines stating that Liam Gallagher had been knifed to death in a brawl with a 'fan'. Being a former Oasis fan, Indra bought a copy of the *Daily Mirror*, and thought it would be something to take his mind off his illness, and when he left the shop he headed for home, which was a flat on Falkner Street.

Upon reaching the junction of Hope Street, he noticed that the modern street 'sculpture' – A Case History – a collection of concrete casts of suitcases and luggage near the former Liverpool Art College – was nowhere to be seen. Indra walked on to his flat on Falkner Street, and when he reached the house in question, he discovered that his key would not fit the lock. He decided he'd have to buzz the number of the old Swedish woman who lived underneath his flat – Number 3. He pressed the button, and a gruff male voice answered. 'Hello?' said the unknown man.

'Hi, is Ingrid there? It's Indra,' the student said into the intercom.

There was a pause as Indra heard the faint white noise hiss from the intercom speaker.

'No. You've got the wrong address, mate,' a crotchety voice replied, and with a click the intercom became silent.

Indra looked at the label next to button number 3 – but it didn't say Ingrid's surname; instead it said 'FLAT 3 – M. MURRAY'. Indra had never heard of anyone of that surname living in any of the neighbouring flats, and he looked at the number on the door, just to make sure he hadn't gone to the wrong house. No, he was at the right house, of course, and this really puzzled him. He put his key in the door once again, but it wouldn't turn. He walked away from the house, utterly confused. He heard a noise coming from above, and when the student looked up, he saw the face of a shaven-headed man of about 50 looking from Ingrid's window at him with a suspicious expression. Indra walked on, and things became even stranger. When he reached Hope Street, he took out his mobile phone and decided to call his former girlfriend Vanessa. She answered the call and when Indra began to tell her about the mysterious disappearance of Ingrid, Vanessa said: 'I think you've got the wrong number.'

'No, it's me, Indra,' the student told her with a smile.

'Who, sorry?' Vanessa asked.

'Indra,' he laughed, and then added, 'have you been drinking?'

'I haven't a clue who you are,' Vanessa said.

'It's me … Indra! Your ex. Stop messing about. I've just …'

Vanessa hung up. Indra called her again. The phone rang for a while and then the automated voice irritatingly announced: 'The person you are calling is not available.'

As Indra swore to himself, he happened to look up. Immediately he noticed there was something wrong with the Anglican Cathedral. Instead of the usual squarish shape of the building's tower, it was much longer and rounded at the top, and the stonework looked much darker, as if it had been subjected to the type of long-term air pollution that once turned the Liver Building and St George's Hall soot-black. This didn't make any sense at all. Indra had passed the cathedral just two days ago and it had looked exactly as it always did, and it was impossible for builders to have altered the shape of the cathedral since then, so what was going on? An eerie thought crossed Indra's disoriented mind: had he died and somehow passed into some parallel world? That would explain why the street sculpture had vanished and also throw some light on the sudden disappearance of his Swedish neighbour. And it could explain why

Vanessa, a girl he had dated for four years, had never heard of him. Indra wandered back into town, and decided to visit a café he often frequented on Bold Street. He was greatly relieved when the people running the café welcomed him. 'How are things, Indra?' said Di, one of the waitresses as he walked in.

'Oh, not so bad,' Indra replied, taking his usual window seat. 'But I've been having some really bad headaches.'

Di loved talking about medical matters, and after she had asked Indra to move his head in certain directions, and felt his neck and looked into his eyes and asked him if he was eating okay, she gave him a bill of clean health. 'You know what you've got?' she said to him, as she went to make his cappuccino.

'No,' said Indra, fearing she'd say 'cancer of the brain' or something.

'Sinusitis,' Di said from the other side of the counter. 'My sister had it really bad. Had nose bleeds and everything.'

'I had them! That's what I had!' Indra said, rising from his seat. He went over to the counter and discussed all of his symptoms with the petite blonde, and she nodded at each new piece of information.

'Just go to your doctors, Indra, or even go to Holland and Barrett and get these ...' Di ripped a page from her orders pad and wrote down the name of two products with which she believed the student could effectively treat his sinusitis.

'Oh, thanks, Di,' Indra said gratefully as she handed him the scribbled note. 'I'd marry you if you weren't already spoken for.'

Di blushed and said she wasn't spoken for. She was single.

Indra went cold, what did she mean? He had met Di's husband and had even bought her three-year-old daughter an ice cream when he bumped into her and her family at the Albert Dock the previous summer.

Indra gave a troubled smile and sat down in the window seat as Di gave him the eye, still blushing. She asked him if he was still with that girl he had come into the café with a few months ago. Indra assumed she was talking about Vanessa, and he said, 'Ah, so you remember her then?'

'Yes, she was very pretty. I could tell her hair was naturally red. Are you not with her now then?'

Indra was puzzled at Di's remarks about his red-headed girlfriend, because Vanessa's hair was raven black, and she had never once dyed it. Four women, all office workers in their thirties who were known to Di, came into the café and she served them, and then she brought over Indra's cappuccino, and went to talk to him, but one of the office workers distracted Di and called over to her. Indra only took a few sips of his coffee before leaving the money on the table and heading for the door.

'You got to go?' Di asked, with disappointment in her eyes.

Indra nodded, and before he stepped out on to Bold Street, he said: 'I'll probably pop back in later, Di.'

'Oh, okay then, bye, Indra,' Di said, and went to collect his money from the table.

Indra walked down Bold Street and went into the Holland & Barrett health store to buy the items Di had recommended for his sinusitis. Upon leaving the health shop, he then decided to call into Waterstones. It was a random choice, brought about by the confusion he felt at the events that were unfolding behind him. He decided he would go upstairs to the coffee shop on the first floor and take the pills he had just bought. The ground floor was packed with people, young and old, and they were all gathered around a table where author Robin Brown was signing copies of his book, which was called *Liverpool is Haunted*. Indra saw that the book's design looked very similar to the *Haunted Liverpool* books in both font and graphical style, as well as thickness. Then came a shock which stunned the student.

Among the people standing around waiting for a signed copy of *Liverpool is Haunted*, was Craig, who had been a college friend of Indra's for three years. Craig had been born with cerebral palsy, and was wheelchair bound – and yet, here he was, standing up, and his hair now had a slight reddish tinge to it. But what really shocked Indra was the presence of the young man standing next to Craig. He was an old friend of his named Barry, who had died in a car crash five years previously – and yet here he was, as large as life, admittedly looking slightly older but in a very healthy and tanned condition. In a voice quivering with emotion, Indra called out his previous best friend's name. 'Barry?' he said, but Barry didn't react. It was as if he hadn't heard him. So Indra moved in closer and tentatively raised his hand to tap Barry on the shoulder. Barry turned to look at him with an expression that was a mixture of annoyance and bafflement.

'Sorry?' Barry said.

'I thought … I thought you were dead, Barry … that terrible crash …' Indra said, and he could feel tears welling up in his eyes.

Barry looked him up and down and swore at Indra, telling him to go away.

Indra recoiled in shock at the profanity, and backed away and out of Waterstones. Indra hurried up Bold Street, breathing heavily, his heart pounding. He passed the café where Di worked, and moments later, he heard a female voice call out his name. Indra halted, and turned. A beautiful young woman with long straight red hair stood there. Could she possibly have called his name?

'Where are you going?' she asked.

Indra slowly realised that this was the 'pretty' girl Di had referred to. In this version of reality, she was his girlfriend.

'I was just going home,' Indra said, and found himself stuck for words.

'How can you be if you're going in that direction?' the redhead asked, and she smiled.

'I live in that direction,' Indra told her. He looked at her beautiful face and figure. She was absolutely perfect.

'What are you talking about, we live down at the dock,' she said, and she beckoned Indra towards her with her curling index finger. Indra walked towards her, and as he came nearer she said: 'I've told you to stop buying things for me; you don't have to.'

Indra could smell her lovely perfume now, and he saw the blueness of her eyes, and the cute freckles which her foundation couldn't hide. She embraced him, kissed his cheek and hugged him hard, then led him by his hand into the café, where Di the waitress gave him daggers. The couple sat in the window seat, and the unknown red-haired girl talked and talked without giving Indra a chance to say anything. His 'partner' stopped chatting at one point and said, 'Aw, your nose is bleeding,' and she dabbed his nose with a napkin.

The vivid bright scarlet blood dripped on to the front of Indra's tee-shirt.

'You'd better go and clean up,' the girl told him, and Indra rose from the table and went to the toilets downstairs. He looked in the mirror above the wash basin and asked himself, 'What the hell is going on?'

And that tingling sensation returned in his head. He shuddered, and gripped the rim of the porcelain basin. He somehow knew that everything had now returned to normal, and one part of him hoped that the beautiful girl with red hair would still be around upstairs – but when Indra went back up, he saw that the window seat was now empty. He looked for his copy of the *Daily Mirror*, but it was nowhere to be seen, and through the window, he saw a rain-slicked Bold Street. Passers-by were hurrying along in the downpour. Indra turned to look for Di, and a waitress named Angela told him that she was on a short holiday and not due in till next week. Angela then said, 'I didn't see you come in before. Have you just come up from the toilet?'

Indra nodded, and his sadness showed in his face. He ordered a cappuccino and sat down and thought hard and long about the mysterious goings-on of the past few hours. He tried to rationalise what he had experienced but was unable to make any sense of it all. He recalled the tabloid headlines about the death of Liam Gallagher, and asked Angela if she knew anything about it. She said she didn't, but took out her phone and searched Google News for any items about the Oasis vocalist, but there was no news of his death listed.

When Indra returned to his flat on Falkner Street, he saw that Ingrid's surname was listed on the intercom, and on this occasion, his key fitted the door. He phoned Vanessa as soon as he got to his flat, and she answered and said, 'Hiya, Indra, what's up?'

He told her about all of the strange incidents – of seeing Craig walking about without his wheelchair and of meeting Barry, five years after he had died in an horrific car crash. Vanessa sounded very concerned and urged Indra to see a doctor. 'No, I'm fine, really,' Indra reassured her, 'the nosebleeds were just because of sinusitis.'

Vanessa was so worried about Indra's mental health, she paid him a visit within the hour and nagged him until he agreed to go to the A&E department of the Royal Teaching Hospital. His head was x-rayed and then a specialist treated him for a rare form of sinusitis which was managed with several pills over a few months. The headaches and nosebleeds never returned. Vanessa began to date Indra again, and the student began to have a series of strange dreams about the red-haired girl he had somehow encountered from some parallel version of his life. Indra would often wake up in tears, because he found that, if he was honest, he loved the girl from his 'other life' more than Vanessa and felt she was his true soulmate. The dreams eventually became less frequent, and today, Vanessa and Indra are happily married. Indra mentioned the strange 'slip' into what seems to have been some alternate life to Di, and she confirmed what he already knew; the waitress had never set eyes on any red-headed girlfriend of his. Perhaps this red-haired beauty exists in this version of Indra's life but maybe her path and his have simply never crossed.

I am a great believer in parallel worlds – versions of our planet that are dislocated dimensionally from this world but sometimes overlapping, allowing us to visit them. These alternative worlds may be the places we glimpse in dreams where we discover people who are dead in our world, walking about in the dream world. Perhaps there are – as quantum physics hints – an infinite number of planet Earths which we could one day visit, where slightly different versions of ourselves and others exist. As you read this book, another version of you may be reading the same book in a world close by in time and space. In that world, the *Titanic* sits in some Californian harbour as a floating museum (having never hit that fatal iceberg in 1912); President Kennedy was never assassinated; and the Beatles never broke up; and you are married to someone else.

Parallel worlds are a fascinating possibility, and may well be proven to exist one day.

ANONYMA

Late one night in the summer of 2002, a young couple entered Central Station on Ranelagh Street and rode the escalator down to the platform where the train would take one of them under the river to Wirral's Eastham Rake. The time was 11.25pm and the train as due any minute. Hannah stood on her tiptoes to kiss the face of her six foot two inch boyfriend Brandon. As the couple, both aged seventeen, embraced, Brandon thought he heard something to his left. The platform was deserted except for a drunken old man who had been talking to himself, and he was to the left of Brandon. Brandon broke away from his lover's kiss for a moment to turn to face the black mouth of the tunnel.

'The train comes from the other direction,' Hannah told him.

'I know,' Brandon replied, and he squinted at the arch of darkness with its ruby red light and a line of grimy neon panel lamps which stretched into a curve. 'I thought I heard a whistling sound.'

'Mmm, come here, you,' Hannah grabbed the collar of his tee shirt and dragged Brandon down to her level to continue the kissing. This time she broke off the kiss, shot a startled look at her boyfriend of three months, then turned her face left. 'Oh yeah, I heard it then,' she said. 'What is it?'

As the two teenagers looked towards the gaping tunnel, they saw three faint white spots floating towards them. As these things got nearer, Hannah thought they resembled dandelions, and Brandon said, 'Are they daddy-bunchies?'

Hannah giggled and said, 'What's a daddy bunchy?'

Brandon blushed and said, 'They're like sort of dandelions and they eat sugar, or at least that's what my Nan used to say.'

'Dandelions aren't alive, you twit,' laughed Hannah, 'they're just fluffy things that come off plants with seed thingies in them.'

Brandon wasn't listening. He had a look of terror in his eyes that made Hannah swing her face to the left again to see what was frightening him. The 'dandelions' were flying about like white bumble bees now, and making a faint whistling sound as they darted through the air. 'What are they?' she gasped.

'Let's go, come on!' Brandon said, with a mounting sense of foreboding, and he backed away towards the wide corridor leading to the escalators.

'They're just flies, Brandon,' said Hannah, resisting his pulls, 'and I'll miss my train, you soft get!'

'They're not flies! Arrgh!' Brandon ducked. One of the white things whizzed within inches of his head and hit the Perspex cover of a tubeway advert with a clicking sound. These things sounded as if they had a hard shell.

Hannah let out a yelp, and then she tried to put her arms up her back – they way people do when they are trying to scratch that itchy part of the back that's almost out of reach. 'Ouch it bit me!' she yelled. 'And it's on me still!'

Brandon put his hands on her shoulders and spun her round. She was wearing a black Pantera tee shirt, and there on the centre of her back, clinging to the shirt, was a white thing that looked just like a dandelion, but each of the 'arms' was hard like a needle, and the needles that were stuck into Hannah's back were red – as if they were miniature transparent hair-thin tubes siphoning off her blood. Hannah let out a string of swear-words and screamed in agony as Brandon tried to pull the barbed creature off her back. The lad let out an agonising cry as the razor-like hairs of the thing dug painfully into his index finger and thumb as he tried to grab it.

'Get it off me!' Hannah sobbed, and seemed ready to faint as she staggered forward. She crumpled on to her knees and her hands rested on the rubbery black-grey tiles of the floor. Brandon took his orange railway ticket from his jeans pocket, and bent it in two, and then he got the ghastly unidentified thing between the folded ticket and at last, managed to pull it out. He tried to throw it on to the track, but the creature flew off – back towards the tunnel from which it had come.

Hannah lay on the floor, crying, and Brandon helped her up then lifted her shirt. Blood was trickling down the long bulge of her spine from the small cluster of tiny incisions. Brandon dabbed at the droplets of blood which kept popping out of the tiny wounds but they wouldn't stop bleeding. The train arrived, and Brandon insisted that he should accompany Hannah home because of the state she was in. Even after the girl had reached her home, the wound was still pouring with blood, and wouldn't stop bleeding until almost one in the morning.

Other people have encountered these 'bloodthirsty dandelions' over the years. A construction engineer on a Liverpool One building site once told me how, in 2008, he saw something white and fluffy drift past him like a snowflake, and then he felt something sting his right cheek. Another white airborn object had inflicted a cut to the engineer's face, and it looked just like the fluffy seed ball of a dandelion. It floated towards Church Street, and seemed to be under intelligent control at one point.

I mentioned this incident and the one which had taken place on the underground on a radio station, and later received a letter from a man named Hammond who said he had studied these unidentified creatures – which he termed 'Anonyma' (derived from the word anonymous) – for many years, and he was of the opinion that some of them were alien and others manmade; created in laboratories by scientists who were meddling with DNA. I do not believe Mr Hammond is a crank. Even the most prominent scientists are discovering new species of microbes all the time, and some viruses which have come to light are providing microbiologists with a headache.

A case in point is the virus that was originally labelled the Bradford coccus, discovered by Timothy Rowbotham, a microbiologist working for the UK's Public Health Laboratory Service. In 1992, Rowbotham was attempting to trace the source of an outbreak of pneumonia in Bradford, and the trail led him to sample some water at the base of a hospital cooling tower. He took his samples back to his laboratory and discovered that they contained amoebae, and the amoebae seemed to have been infected with something – and this something was thought to be a microbe which Rowbotham had never encountered before, so he called it the Bradford coccus. With more pressing matters to attend to, the microbiologist put the Bradford coccus into deep freeze and there it remained for eleven years, until a fresh pair of eyes with an electron microscope took another look at it, and what they saw was astounding.

The Bradford coccus was a freak of nature. It is an unheard-of giant – thirty times bigger than the rhinovirus – and what's more, it is very hard to kill. It looks alien. It seems to be a bacterium, but it isn't, even though it passed the established test for bacteria – the Gram stain. This is a widely used test in which various chemicals are applied to the sample which is suspected of containing bacteria. If the stain produced is purple, then it's a bacterium, if it is pink it is something else. The Bradford coccus produced a purple stain, as if it was a bacterium. The Gram stain test, named after the Danish bacteriologist who first described it – Hans Gram (1853-1938) is generally seen as an infallible method to differentiate bacteria from other forms of life – and yet this test was telling the scientists that a virus was actually a bacterium. The most eminent bacteriologists in the world took a closer look at the Bradford coccus, and all agreed that it was a giant virus. In human terms, imagine a man standing next to a giant who is twelve storeys high – that's the size difference with this strange virus. The head of the giant virus is a polyhedron having twenty planes or faces (which makes it an icosohedron) and it contains 1,262 complex genes in a finely structured body. Most viruses have only between 10 and a 100 genes.

To this day, no one knows what the Bradford coccus is – it may be an virus alien to this planet or perhaps some missing link between viruses and bacteria, but perhaps it forms part of that shadowy group of unidentified creatures Hammond terms as Anonyma. This mysterious group could include the Surrey Puma, the Beast of Bodmin, the Loch Ness Monster, Sasquatch, the Yeti and so on, as well as some of the more local unidentified creatures I have detailed in the *Haunted Liverpool* books: the ghastly-looking snake-like insect with no eyes and razor teeth which lived in the rubbish chute of various tenements in Liverpool in the 1960s, the tripodal creatures that were alleged to have attacked people across the city in the 1970s (see the chapter entitled 'Parasitic Things' in *Haunted Liverpool 17*), as well as the dandelion-like spores that inflict wounds.

THE MINT GREEN CAR

This story came my way many years ago when I first started to collect strange tales. I have had to change a few of the details but I can assure you that, unfortunately, all of the events described in the account happened exactly as I describe them here. But I am at a loss to offer a rational explanation regarding these incidents, though I'm sure some readers will form their own theories in this respect.

Around the mid-Seventies, there stood a used cars lot in Liverpool, not a stone's throw from Seel Street, and it was run by a very atypically honest man in his sixties named Vince. With his pencil thin moustache and prominent gap between his front teeth, Vince bore a certain resemblance to the ultra-debonair actor Terry Thomas.

One beautifully sunny day in early March, Johanna, a twenty-year-old secretary – who went by the shortened form of Jo – visited the used car lot, with its tricolour bunting and a six-foot-tall Michelin tyre man wearing a sandwich board bearing the name 'Vince's Used Cars' upon it. Vince had his back turned to Jo as he was in the middle of a blazing row with a long-haired man of about thirty who wore a denim jacket and a matching pair of jeans. He was saying to Vince, 'I want a refund,' and other things Jo couldn't make out because Vince was talking over the disgruntled customer's heated comments. The blonde secretary found it all quite amusing, even the colourful language, and as the men argued away, Jo went to look for a car. She'd recently passed her test and was in a very good mood. The Equal Pay Act had been passed a few months before and that meant her salary was now the same as her male counterparts – a significant wage-rise in Jo's circumstances: she now earned £3,500 per year. Jo decided on a mint green car at the lot – but it had no price on it. She reasoned that surely the car she wanted could not be more than the one that looked like the same model next to it in pillar box red, which had an asking price of £150. By now, Vince had begrudgingly given the dissatisfied customer his money back, and was shaking his head with dismay as the denim-clad man strutted off.

'How much is this car?' Jo asked, and Vince's jaw dropped when the secretary directed his attention to it.

'That one's a ton, love,' Vince replied, and then seemed suddenly stuck for words.

'A what, sorry?'

'A hundred quid ... er, pounds, miss,' Vince told her, but then he gave a feeble attempt at a smile and said: 'But look at this one here – in romantic red – and only £150. It's more reliable; only had one previous owner you see.'

'I want the mint green one,' Jo insisted, 'I don't like that type of red, it's too gaudy, too showy.'

'Yes, but, well, I'll tell you what, seeing as you're a petite lady, how about that Egyptian-blue mini over there? I wouldn't even mind that car myself to be quite honest ...'

'Well take it then,' Jo replied, quick as a flash, 'because I'll have the mint green car. Now how much did you say? A hundred pounds?'

'Very well, miss. I tell you what ... just give me eighty, okay?' Vince seemed a little sad as he said this. Jo had the feeling he liked the car for some reason and didn't want to part with it.

'What model is it?' Jo asked, stroking the bonnet – which felt warm. It wasn't just warm from the feeble English March sun, but it smelt warm as well – as if the car had been in use just minutes ago.

'It's a Hillman,' Vince told her, watching Jo reach into her handbag for her purse. 'A Hillman Super Imp.'

Jo giggled. 'Imp?'

'Yes, don't let the name fool you though; does eighty, no problem, and it's got a very nice 875c.c. engine – rear mounted as well. You'll get about forty-five miles to the gallon, and it seats four. Real luxurious car. Wish you'd take the red one though; you deserve it before someone else snaps it up.'

Jo handed him the money. 'No thanks, this one will do just fine.'

She signed a form and received the log book, and then she climbed into the car, beamed a huge smile of satisfaction to Vince, and drove off. No more buses, Jo thought, and she also recalled that invitation from her cousin down in Cornwall to stay in that lovely cottage. Now getting there wouldn't involve train tables and taxis. Jo lived off Wavertree Road, and wasn't sure whether to drive straight home to show the car off to her neighbour, Winnie, or whether to drive round for a bit first. She had to go for a spin; it was irresistible. She drove up Renshaw Street, turned left at Lewis's Corner, and followed the H5 bus (which had come from Warrington) at a sensible stopping distance, just like she'd been taught, as it curved from Ranelagh Street into Church Street. She checked the fuel gauge; the tank was half full. Not bad. Then she noticed that the glove compartment was slightly open, and she opened the little door of the compartment further – to reveal a pair of orange knickers. What a weird and rather revolting item to find in a glove compartment, Jo thought …

Beeeeeep!

A Morris Minor from Hanover Street cut in front of Jo and the driver was beeping his horn manically. She swore at him, checked her mirrors, then slowed down outside the Dolcis shoe store on Church Street. She looked at the orange knickers with a smirk, and then closed the compartment tightly, indicated, then turned right into Parker Street, where she passed Owen Owen and soon found herself in busy traffic on Lime Street. She arrived at the junction just before Commutation Row, intending to travel right up London Road, where a policeman wearing a white coat and gloves stood in a raised box directing the traffic. He beckoned Jo and she swerved into London Road, passing Burton the tailors, Jerome's the photographers and of course, TJ Hughes. That store was a real distraction to Jo, who was a complete shopaholic, always on the lookout for bargains, but she had to try her best to concentrate on the road. Anyway, Jo arrived back home at her terraced house off Wavertree Road, and showed the car off to her fifty-five-year-old neighbour Winnie. Jo had only left home a year ago and had known Winnie for just under twelve months. Winnie was very motherly towards her and forever giving advice, and on this particular day, her advice shocked Jo. When Winnie saw the mint green car, she said, 'Jo, I know this sounds funny, but I have a really horrible feeling about that car.'

'Why?' said Jo, understandably made anxious by her friend's concern. 'What do you mean?'

Winnie seemed very upset. 'There's just something about it. I'm sorry, Jo, I wouldn't say anything like this normally; I'd keep it to myself, but I have a really bad feeling about that car.'

Winnie had something of a reputation in her street for being psychic. She also read tea leaves and had made various predictions over the years which had come to pass. Jo had heard about Winnie's alleged psychic abilities, and this made her very uneasy about driving about in the car – but she tried to dismiss all the talk of bad feelings as mumbo-jumbo.

Three days later, Jo was driving back from an old school friend's house in Widnes, and ended up driving home along a very lonely narrow lane which would take her through the farmland and fields of Tarbock Green. The lane was not lit, and was darker still that summer evening because high hedges bordered the lane on each side. As Jo travelled along this lane at about forty miles an hour, she thought she felt the Hillman Super Imp jolt for a moment, as if someone was moving heavily in the vehicle. Around this time, Jo also realised she had not put on her seatbelt, and decided not to divert her attention from the narrow road at that moment in order to put it on – even though she knew that wearing a seatbelt or not could be a matter of life or death; she thought about Jimmy Saville's 'Clunk Click every trip' TV advertising campaign, highlighting the importance of seatbelt safety, and she smiled inanely.

Just then she detected a strong aroma of tobacco, and because the side windows were open on this humid summer evening, Jo wondered if she had passed a place where someone had been smoking, but she had a horrible feeling that there was a smoker actually in the car. As she had just begun to consider the possibility that someone might have sneaked into the car to lie in wait for her as it was parked outside her friend's house, she felt a cold clammy hand being cupped hard over her mouth. Jo reacted to the clamped hand with such shock, she involuntarily turned the wheel and the car almost went through a hedge, but she had the presence of mind to keep the vehicle pointed straight, as the other hand touched her left breast. In the girl's left ear, a gruff voice said, 'Slow down, you bitch!'

Jo slowed down the car, then brought it to a halt, all the while struggling to breathe with the hand pressed against her lips, and she looked into the rear view mirror to see a man with black curly hair, mad staring eyes, and thick eyebrows that met above his long prominent nose.

The man climbed over into the front passenger seat and suddenly produced a knife. He told Jo to recline her seat, and when she looked at the knife in shock, he lifted it as if he was about to plunge it into her chest, and she screamed.

The uninvited passenger then adjusted Jo's seat so she was laying back at about forty-five degrees. She then heard him unzip his trousers and start to unfasten the buckle of his belt as he grinned. 'Just be a good girl and I won't have to stick ya, will I?'

'I've got money if you want that instead,' Jo told the would-be rapist in a trembling voice.

'No thanks, I'll just have you instead,' said the disgusting predator. 'Take your stuff off, now!'

'Please don't! You can have the car as well if you want!' Jo said, and she started to cry.

'I could kill you and still do it you know!' the man screeched, and his breath reeked of Golden Virginia tobacco.

Just then, Jo noticed a light in the nearside mirror. Another vehicle was approaching. It was a Liverpool man in his thirties named Paul Harris, returning from his girlfriend's house in Widnes on his prized 200c.c. Ariel Arrow motorcycle.

'Stay still or I'll cut your throat wide open,' the rapist warned Jo, but she slyly reached for the handle on the door, and waited for a few seconds, wondering if she'd soon be dead. She hadn't put her seatbelt on, so there was a chance she'd be able to sprint out of the car as soon as she opened the door. She suddenly pushed the door open and almost fell out of the vehicle into the hedge, before running down the road towards the motorcyclist waving her arms in the air as the rapist turned the air blue behind her with some of the coarsest language she had ever heard.

Paul Harris slowed down and came to a halt about ten feet away from Jo. She ran to him and told him how a man with a knife had tried to rape her, and she tried to climb on to the motorbike, but Paul pushed her back, and rolled the motorcycle to the side of the road, where he kicked the stand down. He took off his crash helmet, and crept up on the mint green car with the helmet held up slightly, as if he intended to strike the rapist with it. Paul looked in the Hillman and saw nobody there.

'Be careful! He's got a knife!' Jo warned him in an hysterical voice.

'There's no one in here, love,' Paul told her, and he even knelt down and looked under the car. He then walked to the hedge at the side of the road and checked to make sure that no one could have passed through it. He naturally wondered if the girl who had flagged him down was some kind of attention seeker or was even deranged. 'Well, he's vanished into thin air.'

'He must still be in there!' Jo said, and started to cry.

Paul came up to her and said, 'Look, I swear there is no one in that car. Now, are you going to Liverpool?'

'Yes,' Jo replied, and wiped her eyes, which were now streaked with mascara.

'Well look, I'll drive behind you all the way … how's that?' Paul proposed.

'Are you absolutely sure he's gone?' Jo asked, looking at the car with pure dread.

Paul nodded and patted her left shoulder in a very reassuring manner. 'I'd bet my life on it, love. So get in your car now, and I'll go with you, and then I'll escort you home.'

And true to his word, Paul escorted Jo all the way to her home on Wavertree Road, and even came in to have a cup of tea with her and Winnie.

That night, Jo had a series of nightmares about the rapist, and in the morning as she was eating her cornflakes, she kept going over the assault in her mind, trying to rationalise just how the assailant could have entered the car. He must have sneaked in as it was parked outside of cousin's home in Widnes, Jo thought, but even if that was the case, how had he escaped from the car after she had flagged down Paul Harris?

Jo felt uneasy about venturing into that car for the rest of that day, but on the following morning, the bright Spring sunshine seemed to partly evaporate her fears of the previous evening. Jo decided that the would-be rapist was probably just some opportunist; there was nothing supernatural or weird about his presence in the vehicle. She drove to her workplace off Dale Street, and at the end of the usual never-ending typing and Tippexing shift, she set off for home, braving the madness of the rush hour traffic. She reached home at 5.25pm, after stopping off for a mixed grill at a chippy on Wavertree Road, just around the corner from her place. Jo had had a bit of a falling out with her mother six months ago. Her mum had wanted her to stay at home until she found a decent boyfriend rather than living alone at her own place, and Jo, being the fiercely independent girl she was, deliberately went out and rented a place as far from her Litherland home as possible. But now Jo wondered how her mum – and dad – were doing, and so, on a spur of the moment whim, she decided to drive up to her parents' house on Litherland's Hatton Hill Road. Jo intended to set out on the eight-mile journey at 7pm, but she received a visit from an old school friend, Joyce, at 6.40pm, and the two girls chatted and caught up on each other's lives, and this delayed her trip. Jo was only too eager to show off her car to Joyce, and she drove her friend to her home in the Dingle that evening at 8pm, and only then embarked on the journey to Litherland. Twilight was falling by now, and darkness seemed to be gathering by the very minute, which naturally made Jo a little edgy, because she was mindful of the similar lighting conditions when she had been attacked the night before. Joyce had told Jo she should have reported the attack to the police, and Jo shook her head and said she was frightened the would-be rapist would come after her if she did that. She just wanted to forget the whole thing.

As Jo was driving up along Derby Road towards Bootle, a strange silence seemed to creep over everything. To the left stood towering grim warehouses with their dark windows, and it was upon this stretch of road that something terrifying took place. Once again Jo thought she could smell tobacco inside the vehicle. She tried to remember if Joyce had smoked in the car when she had driven her home. No, she was sure she hadn't. She had definitely smoked in her house, her usual Players No. 6 – but this aroma was undoubtedly the same tang as the Golden Virginia tobacco she had smelt seconds before the attack.

Jo shot a glance in her rear view mirror.

It was him – again. He was leaning forward in the back seat, but he wasn't looking at Jo; he was watching the passing warehouses as if he was fascinated with their dark facades. Jo pulled up at the traffic lights, undid her safety belt, and jumped out of the car. A car horn beeped and tyres screeched behind her as cars braked hard to avoid knocking her down. Jo heard the man in her car shout after her: 'No you don't! Come back here!'

But she hurried across the road without even knowing where she was going, as she didn't know this part of the city that well. She walked up Millers Bridge in a daze, convinced by now that the man who had attempted to rape her was some kind of ghost. There was no other explanation. Jo waved frantically to a policeman on the other side of the road, and when he came over to see what the matter was, she told him what had happened, but thought it would be unwise to tell him about the previous assault. The police converged on the abandoned Hillman Super Imp, and found no one in it. but nothing anyone could say could persuade her to get back in that car, and it was sold for £50 via the used cars column of the *Liverpool Echo*. Out of curiosity, Jo went back to Vince's Used Car lot, and asked the jovial dealer if that car had a history. 'I don't know what you're talking about,' he said.

Jo told him it had been haunted, without giving him any other details.

'Haunted?' said Vince with a sham chuckle, then asked: 'Well that's a new one, love. You saying you want your money back? Because you can't get a refund on the basis that something is haunted. I don't remember seeing anything about that in the trade descriptions act.'

'Oh, don't worry, I've already sold it,' Jo told him, observing the nervous behaviour of the dealer with suspicion, 'but I just wondered if you knew there was something odd about that car.'

Vince raised his eyebrows, feigned a look of innocence, and shrugged. 'As far as I'm concerned it was a perfectly decent car,' he claimed.

'Nah, I think you knew that car had a ghost,' Jo told him, looking Vince right in the eyes. 'That's why you wanted to sell me that red one instead, isn't it? And I'll bet that bloke you were arguing with the day I bought the car – the one you gave the money back to – had discovered that car was haunted. I'm right, aren't I?'

Vince turned and walked away and went into his hut without saying a word.

In 1997, a woman from Kirkdale named Sarah told me that she had once owned an old green car which she had used as a runaround after she had passed her test in 1976. Whenever this woman drove at night, she said she would start to smell pungent tobacco and then she would feel the 'presence' of someone male in that cab. Sarah had the feeling that this unseen man was violent, and she felt quite threatened when the presence manifested itself. After just a few weeks, Sarah gave the car to a friend. I asked Sarah how she had come into possession of the green car, and she said she had bought it for £50 via the used cars column of the *Liverpool Echo* from a woman in Wavertree ...

WHO'S THAT GIRL?

In the summer of 2009 a rather strange and eerie daylight haunting took place off Townsend Lane and Breck Road. It all started when a forty-five-year-old Donna left her terraced home on Empress Road, off Townsend Lane, in the Cabbage Hall district of the city. Divorcee Donna was going in search of her boyfriend of fifteen months, a fifty-year-old man nicknamed 'Buster', who originally hailed from Speke. Buster was normally a selfless man; although a rough diamond in some ways, and never shy when it came to using his fists, should trouble come his way, but that was only one side of him, and Donna and her seventeen-year-old daughter Avril had come to love Buster in the short time they had got to know him, but every now and then, Buster would go out for a packet of cigarettes and embark on a never-ending pub-crawl.

On this sunny day in July 2009, Buster had gone out in the morning to buy twenty cigarettes and a magazine for Avril, and somewhere along the way, he had bumped into his old friend Gerry Curtayne, and Donna's neighbour Julie had seen the two men talking near Ugly Ben's recycled furniture shop on Townsend Lane, so Donna guessed that Buster and his old school chum had probably gone for a drink in the Stadium pub further up the lane. And so as Donna and Avril strolled up Townsend Lane, various friends and neighbours – some of them nosy parkers and gossipers – and some of them people who genuinely cared for Donna and her daughter – asked where Buster was. Donna had to lie to some of those who were forever spreading gossip about her (and even about Avril). Donna told them Buster had gone for a drink with a relative who was visiting from Scotland, although Avril almost gave the game away by smirking as her mum told these little white lies. Avril thought she saw Buster coming out of Mio's Mini Market, but it was just someone who looked like him from behind.

As mother and daughter were crossing Clarendon Road, which is a little side street off Townsend Lane, Avril noticed a beautiful little girl of about seven or eight coming out of the mouth of the alleyway at the back of the E G Doors store. This alleyway was gated, as many of the entries in Liverpool and other major cities are nowadays. An alleygate is there to prevent and reduce burglaries, criminal damage by vandals, as well as anti-social behaviour – so Avril assumed that the little girl, who wore a blue gingham dress and had long jet-black hair, had not been down the alleyway, but had probably been playing near the top of the entry just round the corner. She was too small to have been able to climb an alleygate. The little porcelain-skinned child walked towards Donna and Avril, and at closer quarters, Avril was struck by her huge dark blue eyes. She smiled faintly at Avril, and because of her short strides, Donna and her daughter soon outpaced her and overtook her as they headed for the first port of call in their quest for Buster.

'He never drinks in here, Mam,' Avril told her mother, as she halted at the entrance to the Winchester pub. Donna went in anyway and had a quick look around. Whilst her mother was inside, Donna put on the earphones of her iPod and started to listen to some songs. Nearby stood the little girl she'd set eyes on a minute or so ago. She was standing near the doorway to the Ryan & Son Bathroom store, and she seemed transfixed by the iPod. Donna came out, 'He's not in there and no one's seen him anywhere,' she said. 'I hope he hasn't been knocked down or anything.'

So they carried on up Townsend Lane, and as Avril passed an Indian takeaway, she looked back to see that the girl in the blue gingham dress was still standing by the bathroom fittings shop, still looking intently at her. Donna reached the Stadium pub a few minutes later, but Buster was not in there, and nor had any of the drinkers who knew him clapped eyes on him that day. Donna and Avril carried on walking, and coming from the other direction was that little girl again. Donna thought nothing of the child's presence, but Avril wondered how she had managed to travel from that spot outside the bathroom store to the busy junction where Townsend Lane meets Lower Breck Road. The girl smiled at Avril as she passed, then headed north, back in the direction from which Donna and Avril had come, towards the Stadium pub.

Donna was starting to panic, and she and Avril dashed over the roads at the hectic junction and called in at the Cabbage Hall. None of the drinkers had seen Buster, but then an old man named Alf said he had seen Donna's fellah going down Breck Road twenty minutes before with 'some little baldy man' – an accurate description of Gerry Curtayne. Back outside, Donna and Avril recrossed the busy junction and there, on that great triangular green, was the girl in the gingham dress, about fifty yards to Avril's left, apparently following them with her eyes as they quickened their pace towards Holy Trinity church. They had just passed the church, when the little girl jumped out from behind a red post office pillar box and shouted, 'Boo!'

Avril was taken aback by her sudden appearance because she had just seen her further down the road on that green triangle of grass by Lower Breck Road. It was not humanly possible, without any transport, for anyone to travel from that triangle to the pillar box in such a short time. Avril wondered if she was perhaps seeing the girl's twin sister, but when she turned to look down the road, there was no other girl in sight.

Just then a voice called out to Donna from nearby St David's Road. It was her elderly uncle, Chad. When she told him she was looking for Buster and was really worried about him, Chad clutched her hands and said: 'Donna, you're worrying for nothing, girl. I bumped into him before, and he said he's going to a pub called the Round House ... I think he meant the one on Irvine Street, the Mount Vernon. He was with a mate of his ...'

'The Mount Vernon?' Donna tried to remember the pub. She had drunk there many years ago. 'Isn't that sort of at the edge of Kenny, nor far from the hospital?'

'Yeah, you know where Paddy Comp was, don't you?' Chad asked, tracing an imaginary road in the air with the flat of his hand.

'Archbishop Blanch you mean?' Avril chipped in.

'Don't confuse her, Avril,' Chad said, grinning.

'Yeah, I remember where it is now. Ah, thanks, Uncle Chad,' Donna said, and she turned to the roadway as Chad dipped into his wallet and gave Avril a tenner.

'Oi! Taxi!' Donna yelled, and a cab pulled over.

In the taxi, Donna said, 'I wonder why he's gone to the Mount Vernon? You don't think he's seeing someone, do you?'

But Avril wasn't listening; she was looking back at that little girl, who was now standing near the spot where they had met Uncle Chad, staring directly at the taxi. Avril shivered; there was something deeply disturbing about the child, something other-worldly. Her mother's words suddenly registered, 'Nah, Buster's not seeing anyone, Mum. You won't let him go anywhere on his own, so how could he meet anyone?'

'I know I don't, because see what happens when he does go out on his own?' said Donna, trying to justify her possessiveness. 'Hey, you don't think he's gone to meet someone off the internet do you? He's seen you in those chat rooms; it might have given him ideas.'

'Oh, Mum, please shut up and come back into the real world,' was Avril's tetchy reply as she switched on her iPod again.

The taxi soon reached the Mount Vernon pub with its distinctive rounded facade, and Donna and Avril went inside, and there was Buster and his friend Gerry, laughing their heads off over something, but when Buster set eyes on Donna and Avril, his smile quickly faded.

'Did you get your ciggies then?' Donna asked him, and Buster seemed stuck for words.

'Hiya, love, well what it was you see … it's just that … well …'

'Don't "hiya love" me, Bamber,' Donna replied, for once addressing Buster by his real name, which made Avril grin.

'No, wait, give me a word in edgeways, will ya?' Buster told her, and he reached first into his left inside pocket, and then his right inside pocket.

'It's in there,' Gerry said to Buster, and tapped his left coat pocket with the back of his hand.

Buster tapped the pocket and took out a small dark red box. He opened it then got down on one knee in front of Donna. Donna steadied herself by leaning on the vacant tall bar stool, looking as if she was about to cry.

Buster recited Donna's full name – even including her confirmation name – and then asked, 'Will you marry me?'

'Oh, shit!' Avril said unconsciously.

'Yes!' Donna replied, as tears flowed in her eyes and Buster slipped the white-gold engagement ring on to the third finger of her left hand.

'I thought I'd have a drink to steady myself before I asked you, Don,' Buster told her, 'because I was a bag of nerves. That's why I was so restless last night. I'd planned to propose to you in the kitchen when you were making breakfast, but my nerve went.'

There was a wave of 'ahs' from several of the women present – and one from a sarcastic young lad as well.

Drinks were soon flowing, but Avril soon got bored, and wandered outside to phone her friend Melissa and tell her about the 'cheesy marriage proposal' – but outside stood that little girl in the blue gingham dress. Avril recoiled in shock in mid-conversation, and then said nothing for a while. Melissa kept asking her if she was still there. The girl gave a sinister smile, and Avril realised that the blueness of the child's eyes had now turned to black. She turned and ran back into the pub to tell her mother, but by now the jukebox was booming away and Donna and Buster were dancing like two people possessed as the drinkers clapped in time. Avril shouted for her mother to stop dancing but Donna was on another planet, elated at the proposal, and already the gin and tonic was working its magic in her brain. It was useless. Avril went back into the hallway and opened the door a crack. There was no sign of the girl. She cautiously stepped out into the street but the child was nowhere to be seen. The only people about were passers-by and two middle-aged smokers, forced by the Smoking Ban to smoke outside the pub.

At this point, Avril decided to walk home all the way to Empress Road, but every now and then she would catch a glimpse of that little girl. She was undoubtedly a ghost, for she would pop out of phone boxes seconds after Avril had seen her quite a distance away, and she seemed to have the ability to run through alleygates, emerging from the entries of various streets to chase after Avril as she shrieked with laughter. At one point, when Avril finally reached Townsend Lane, she saw the girl standing outside a café called Ann's Pantry. Avril stopped, wondering what she would do next. She ran off down the lane, then sprinted across a patch of grassy wasteland where she seemed to fall. Avril crept past this wasteland and halted for a moment to see where the apparition was. All of a sudden, Avril spied the shadow of the girl's head and shoulders inching along the pavement towards her left. Avril ran across the road to avoid the tormenting apparition, missing certain death by inches as a van flew past her. She stood panting by a carpet store on the corner of Cathedral Road, looking across the road to the girl in the blue dress, who was now standing as still as a statue, her face emotionless. Avril raced off home to Empress Road but diverted to the house of her mum's friend, Julie. Avril was spouting out the seemingly unbelievable account of the creepy stalking girl, when Julie cut in, 'I believe you, Avril, I've seen her myself.'

Julie said she had seen a girl fitting that exact description two years ago, and like now, it had been a fine July day. The girl had followed her as far as Clubmoor where Julie went to see her sister. Julie said a few older people in the street had seen the little girl over the years and the general consensus amongst the elders of the neighbourhood was that the child was the ghost of a little girl who was killed during the Second World War when a German bomb landed on her house. Avril was not a religious person, but felt moved enough to go to church, where she said an 'Eternal Rest' prayer for the earthbound phantom and also lit a candle for the child as a symbolic gesture. After which, she saw no more of the ghost in blue gingham.

SLEEPY GENE

As far-fetched as it may seem, the following story is alleged to be true, and is based on the testimony of three rather simple unpretentious people, one of whom has since died. There have been a few name-changes, but otherwise the story is exactly as it was related to me by the people involved. The story references the well-reported phenomenon of possession.

Sleep is the greatest thief, for he steals a third of your life, yet in sleep, all are equal; what difference is there between Solomon and a fool when both are in slumbers? Even tyrants like Hitler and Stalin spent a third of their life on holiday from their own egos during the hours of sleep. Mystics say that sleep is the brother of death, that just as we cannot remember the exact point of falling asleep, we will one day be equally oblivious about the point when we slip out of this life. But there are many mysteries concerning sleep; are dreams merely fragments of the waking life, or is there more to them than meets the eye? There was a rather strange case that illustrates what I'm referring to, and it all unfolded in Tuebrook in the infernal late summer of 1976, the year of the Great Drought.

On Wednesday, 7 September 1976, at 5.10pm, thirteen-year-old Gene Wilson sat down at the family tea table, and as usual his father Ernie told him off because he would habitually turn his chair towards the television, because his favourite programme was just starting – a Liverpool-based children's drama series called *Rocky O'Rourke*.

The Wilsons were a big family. There was Gene, of course, his sisters, Sue, fifteen, Michelle twelve, Joanne, nine, and brothers Michael, sixteen, Billy, ten, and Gary, six. There was also Nanny Ann Wilson, who was in her seventies. Nanny was a lover of wrestling (especially Mick McManus) bingo and horseracing and would put a bet on, Monday to Saturday. It was her only real pleasure, besides her Harold Robbins books. Then there was her husband, Grandad George Wilson, a very active man of seventy-five who walked miles to the Pier Head and back each day from the family home in Marlborough Road, Tuebrook. Grandad deluded himself into thinking he was Liverpool's answer to the science historian James Burke, there to explain scientific principles and translate anything technological into layman's terms for the family. On this very day in fact, he was babbling on about NASA's Viking 2 Lander probe, which had just touched down on Mars, but no one was listening. 'If the world was the size of a beach ball,' he told Gene, 'Mars would be where the Jolly Miller pub is; that's how far space goes up, like.'

Mrs Wilson told her husband to stop reading the *Liverpool Echo* at the table while they were 'dining' – a word that always made the girls snigger. Mr Wilson sighed, folded the newspaper, and tackled his plate of scouse. Michael and Billy talked about tomorrow's big game at Wembley between England and the Republic of Ireland, in particular the suitability of manager Don Revie, Keegan and Thompson's leg injuries, and who was the best footie player in their school. Sue whispered to Michelle about her ex-boyfriend Richie Ryan, and how he had tried to make her jealous by kissing Maureen 'Spotty' Muldoon on Lorenzo Drive.

Against this typical domestic backdrop, on this particular September day, something very strange took place. After Gene Wilson had finished his scouse, he enjoyed the usual slice of sandwich cake for dessert, and a bottle of Cresta lemonade, before retiring to his room for forty winks on this feverishly warm evening. As the family laughed at the contestants' antics on the television show *It's A Knockout*, downstairs, Gene dozed off for what he expected to be a short nap, but when he awoke, he found himself standing under a full moon in Newsham Park with his arms around a beautiful girl he had never seen before ...

'John, why have you stopped?' Jennifer Danebury asked with a puzzled look in her beautiful eyes.

'Why have I stopped what? And who's John?' Gene Wilson asked, backing away from the girl. What on earth was he doing in a moonlit Newsham Park? he wondered. Was he was still dreaming? No, it all felt too real to be a dream.

'Why have you stopped dancing?' Jennifer asked. There was love in her twinkly eyes, and it scared the virginal Gene. The teenagers gazed at one another in silence for a moment under the full moon, with the distant sounds of traffic and the faint barking of a dog in Rocky Lane heightening the isolation of the park. 'Why has your voice changed?' Jennifer asked. Her face was like porcelain, doll-like, by the light of the moon.

'I've always talked like this,' said Gene, self-consciously, and he turned mumbling, 'anyway I better be getting home. Me Mam'll be looking for me.'

As he hurried away from the girl – who was unknown to him – she shouted after him. 'Why are you going?' But Gene ran off northwards into the cool night, afraid because he thought he'd been sleepwalking. How else could he have ended up in Newsham Park after going to bed? He heard Jennifer's faint voice drifting past him on the night breeze, 'John! Don't go!'

All the way home, Gene wondered who this John was. When he reached his home in Marlborough Road at five-past eleven, he found the front door ajar, all the lights on in the house, but no one about. Then came a blast of sound from the television set – the opening bars of the theme tune to *What the Papers Say* – which startled him. He turned the volume down and then went next door to Mrs Folkestone to see if she knew where everyone had disappeared to.

'Ah, here he is, Barbara!' Mrs Folkestone said, when she opened her front door, and his neighbour ushered him into her back parlour, where most of the Wilson family were gathered. Gene's mother was furious, and his father wanted to have words with him as well, but didn't get a chance. 'Where've you been?' Mrs Wilson shouted, and the boy's sisters also told him off, saying how worried they'd all been after finding his bed empty at 8pm. 'Grandad's still walking the streets looking for you!' fifteen-year-old Sue yelled at Gene. 'Where have you been?'

'I don't know,' Gene confessed, 'I woke up in Newsham Park with my arms around some girl!' immediately realising how ludicrous this must sound.

Gene's little sister, nine-year-old Joanne, formed a perfect 'O' with her mouth, and said 'Aaaah! Have you been going out with a girlfriend without telling Mum and Dad?'

'What girl? Who is she? And what have you been up to, hey?' Mr Wilson wanted to know, but Gene just shook his head and said, 'I just told, you I don't know! I don't know how I ended up in the park!'

'Liar!' said Gene's other sister, twelve-year-old Michelle, and she turned to her mother. 'Mam, I seen him ...' she started to say. 'You *saw* him, Michelle, not *seen* him,' her father corrected the girl.

'Dad!' Michelle squealed, 'I seen, er saw, our Gene leave the house and I asked him where he was going, and he swore at me in a weird voice!'

'I did not!' said Gene emphatically, hurt and confused.

Anyway, at 1am, he finally got to bed after enduring a sermon from his father on the 'right way' to find a girlfriend. As soon as Gene fell asleep that night, 'John' took over his body again.

Gene Wilson slipped out of his bed – or should I say – John Wilson did. John was a thirteen-year-old who had been born in 1701. Through sheer willpower, his spirit had somehow managed to squat in the attic of Gene Wilson's subconscious, and whenever Gene's conscious mind slept, John would take over the cerebellum neurons of his brain. 'Ah! Life!' John rejoiced, inhaling air, once again savouring the delights of being alive in a flesh-and-blood body after being a spirit for 262 years. How was this possible? How could one from the Silent Majority (all the dead and unborn people) simply slip into a living body? Any genuine exorcist will vouch for me when I say that spirits can and occasionally do take over one of the living, but they rarely stay in the living for any duration. John Wilson, however, was able to infiltrate Gene Wilson's mind because his DNA and mindprint were exactly the same as his, due to Gene being a remote descendant of the eighteenth century teen. When John died in a house fire in 1714, he had been about to elope with Jenny Quidhampton – a poor Lancashire farm girl, and in 1976, Jenny's exact replica existed in the form of the Tuebrook schoolgirl Jennifer Danebury.

John Wilson came down from Gene's bedroom and explored the house. Keeping watch in the shadows was nine-year-old Joanne Wilson. She had come down for a glass of water on this unbearably hot summer night, and had hidden when she heard Gene's footsteps. At first she thought it was her brother, but then she heard John Wilson's peculiar voice. 'Ah, milk of human kindness,' he muttered, and chuckled, after opening the fridge door in the kitchen and knocking back a whole pint of Unigate milk. 'Milk, I had forgotten the silken taste of thee. In the dark realm of spirits I had dreamed so long of thee,' John soliloquised, and smiling, wiped the milk from his lips, and sighed as he poked his head into the coolness of the fridge. 'Gloriana! Bread, and butter! Yes, I must have them also.'

Joanne watched from the triangle of darkness under the stairs. What's wrong with Gene? she wondered. She saw him grinning at the Mother's Pride loaf. 'Tis a loaf already sliced, how novel!' he said, and used the huge sharp breadknife to spread butter on the slices of bread. Weird raspy voices could be heard in the air in the kitchen, and they scared Joanne; they were the voices of evil jealous spirits and two mocked John, 'You won't stay alive long, dead man!' whined one, and another deep gruff-voiced spirit warned, 'You'll be punished for entering the world of life!'

John gritted his teeth and swiped the air over the sink with the breadknife – and that really scared Joanne. A tear rolled down her cheek; she wanted the Gene she knew to come back immediately.

John Wilson then left the kitchen and sneaked out of the house, into the night.

Joanne woke her parents, sisters and brothers and told them Gene had gone 'bonkers'. The youngest of the family, six-year-old Gary, didn't understand why everyone was in turmoil, and when he saw the milk bottle John Wilson had emptied on the draining board, the boy chimed out the jingle that was forever advertising milk on the television: 'Watch out, watch out, watch out, watch out, there's a Humphrey about!'

Grandad Wilson requisitioned grandson Michael's Ultraviolet Chopper bike and went in search of Gene, while the three Wilson girls and their mum went to the police station. Gene's father took his sons Michael and Billy with him to search Newsham Park, while little Gary stayed at home with his nan.

Then came some shocking news from a neighbour, which sent Mrs Wilson into a swoon. Her son Gene had been knocked down by a Cortina on West Derby Road, near the junction with Orphan Drive. As the sobbing motorist leaned over Gene, lying inert in the gutter, he saw a ghostly glowing figure of a young man in a huge curly white wig and eighteenth century-type clothes emerge out of the unconscious teen. The motorist understandably fled after the apparition slapped him across the face and called him a 'buffoon' and a word that sounded like 'slubberdegullion'.

The dislodged spirit body of John Wilson then ran off to Newsham Park, for a romantic rendezvous with Jennifer Danebury, the girl for whom he had returned to life. The ambulance arrived and took Gene to hospital, and all of the Wilson family – except Grandad – followed in the neighbour's van. Luckily Gene was only concussed but would be kept in hospital overnight for observation. Grandad Wilson, who was not aware of the accident, ironically passed the ambulance in his search for Gene, and decided to steer the chopper bike into Newsham Park. What he saw at first scared him, but then intrigued him: the glowing eighteenth century counterpart of his grandson.

John Wilson was merrily singing *Greensleeves* as he made his way across the moonlit park to the bridge, where he hoped his lover would be waiting for him. Jennifer Danebury was as romantic as John, but the John she was longing for looked like Gene Wilson, and when she saw the radiant phantom in his huge white 'judge's' wig, embroidered satin coat with turned up sleeves, breeches, and stockings from the knees to his square-toed buckled shoes, she felt dizzy with fear. A real live ghost! She clutched the handrail of the bridge, feeling faint, but John Wilson, suddenly shy, stopped singing *Greensleeves* and fidgeted with the brass buttons of his ethereal coat as approached the petrified girl. 'I hath returned from the grave for thy warm love, fair maiden Jenny!' he managed in a choked voice. 'I have fended off a legion of unclean spirits and braved the Valley of Death to rejoin you! Of all the numberless dead I alone hath returned to the living side of nature to become thine husband.'

'Yer what?' Jennifer gulped, light-headed with shock. John Wilson intended to kiss Jennifer's knuckle but he couldn't lift her hand – because his hand went straight through hers, now that he no longer inhabited Gene Wilson's flesh-and-blood body. With horror, John realised he was but an insubstantial ghost, and the evil, wicked spirits soon arrived and closed in on him. They kicked him viciously, and Jennifer screamed. The shadowy gargoyles rose out of the lake and from every shady spot to torment him. 'Back to the darkness, dead man!' commanded one red-eyed demon with ash-coloured skin.

Grandad Wilson watched the spectacle, and noticed a tall dark figure standing nearby. 'Go and stop them!' said the old man to this silhouette, 'Those thugs are beating him! Stop them!' The grandfather got ready to go to the rescue on the chopper but the dark stranger turned to face the old knight on a bike, and revealed an horrific face with two bright glowing orange eyes and other aspects which lead me to believe that he was Abaddon, the patron demon of hate and destruction. 'Leave here or die!' this entity roared.

Grandad Wilson yelped and hurried off, abandoning the bike. A whirlwind of demonic laughter came down on to the bridge and whisked John Wilson into a spiralling blackness. 'Goodbye, sweet Jenny, goodbye, my love,' he cried, and Jennifer Danebury turned and never stopped running till she reached her Tuebrook home.

HUYTON'S GHOSTLY HIGHWAYMAN

Out of nowhere, an eerie figure in a three-cornered hat and a flowing cape was seen to emerge on horseback from a thick mist early one morning in November 1976. He was coming from the direction of Huyton's Twig Lane towards Cotsford Road. Fifty-five-year-old David had been on his way to Twig Lane, where his friend Ron would pick him up in a transit van to give him a lift to his workplace in Prescot. On this morning, David left his home on Cotsford Road a little earlier than usual (6.50am) because he had accidentally set his alarm clock ten minutes fast. A ground mist blanketed everything up to knee-level and gave a ghostly aspect to the road. As David had left his home he had heard the distinctive clip-clop of a horse somewhere in the distance and thought that perhaps a mounted policeman was in the area – but as he walked up the road he saw the silhouette of the horse; it was a huge animal, like a shire horse in build, and sitting on it was a very alarming figure in a tricorn hat and a long cloak of some sort – and this outdated figure was pointing a gun straight at David as it stood there stock-still. David halted, wondering what to do. His instincts soon told him to turn and run, and as he did so he thought he heard the man on horseback shout, 'Come back!'

David didn't have a telephone landline – and in those days, mobile phones of the type we now use were unheard of – and so he decided to find a phone box and alert the police to the nutter in fancy dress. But was the person really demented, or just perpetrating a hoax? As David approached the phone box, he saw his mate Ron passing in the transit van, so he ran towards him and flagged the vehicle down. Before he could say a word, Ron said, 'There's a fellah up there dressed as a highwayman,' and pointed towards the Liverpool Road end of twig Lane. David then told him how he'd seen the same figure minutes ago and had had a gun pointed at him. The two men then drove up Twig Lane in search of the horseman. David never reported the incident and Ron dropped him off at his Prescot workplace before driving to his own workplace in the Whiston area.

David never mentioned the 'highwayman' to anyone else, but that day at lunchtime in his work canteen, thirty-year-old Stan said his sister had been coming back from her boyfriend's house on Dinas Lane a few nights ago, and heard a horse galloping behind her as she was walking up Lincombe Road. She turned to see a man in a black cloak and 'funny old-fashioned hat', tearing down the road on a giant steed. The man shouted something to her as he galloped past, and then, as he passed Jubilee Park, he vanished into thin air, but the sound of the horse's hooves could still be heard for about half a minute until they eventually faded away.

When David heard of this encounter with the highwayman, he told Stan about his own meeting with what must have been a ghost. About a week after this, David was again on his way to work, only this time there wasn't a trace of any fog about and it was a bright clear sunny morning. As David reached the junction of Twig Lane, he heard the distant sounds of a horse at full gallop, but could not see any horse or ghostly highwayman anywhere.

I have received many reports of the so-called Huyton Highwayman over the years, and from what I can gather, he and his spectral steed have been at large in the Huyton, Page Moss and Whiston areas for many decades. Huyton is, of course, an ancient place, and its name is probably derived from the Anglo-Saxon words 'heah' and 'tun' meaning an elevated enclosure. Huyton is referred as Hitune in the Domesday Book, but the spelling we know today appeared in the thirteenth century. Huyton in the eighteenth century was, like many other rural towns, frequented by highwaymen, including the infamous Black Jack, who terrorised both stagecoaches and lone travellers on the roads between Huyton and Liverpool. For many years a rumour has persisted that a highwayman's treasure lies buried somewhere near Huyton Quarry Station. In 1933, ten silver coins dating from around 1708 were found near the station and since then, many amateur archaeologists and budding treasure hunters have gone in search of the fabled highwayman's treasure.

One rainy evening in 1910, several drinkers leaving the Rose and Crown in Huyton are said to have encountered the ghost of a highwayman and his horse. On that occasion the highwayman rode towards the parish church of St Michael, and was seen to fade away before it reached the cemetery walls. In December of that same year, just before Christmas, the apparition of the highwayman was seen – this time without his horse – standing inside the snow-covered cemetery, and on this occasion, a hooded monk-like figure was standing next to the highwayman, apparently in conversation. A group of children and two elderly men were the witnesses to this intriguing incident.

During excavations around St Michael's Church in 1873, as a wall was being repaired, a stone column (thought to be of Saxon origin) carved with four helmeted heads, was unearthed in the grounds of the church, as well as a sandstone font, both dating from the ninth century. When these discoveries were made, the hooded ghost was seen in the vicinity, and this is often the case when hallowed ground is disturbed; it often triggers paranormal activity. When a Mr H E Smith mentioned the sightings of the ghostly monk to the Historic

Society at their meeting at the Royal Institution in Colquitt Street on 27 November 1873, there were sneers and sniggers all round. Over 130 years later, some still scoff at the idea of ghosts.

In the 1890s, a figure on horseback that looked exactly like the archetypal Dick Turpin type of highwayman was seen riding along on a heavy draft horse on the railway tracks near the level-crossing of Huyton station. On this occasion, the ghost and his horse were seen in broad daylight and dissolve into thin air as many looked on. A few oldsters claimed that this same apparition had been seen back in 1852, minutes before a fatal accident involving one Thomas Sparkes took place in October of that year. Sparkes, of Liverpool, was getting into a carriage as the train was in motion, when he slipped and received such injuries to the feet and ankles, that amputation of both legs below the knee 'was obliged immediately to be made' as the reporter in *The Times* put it. Sparkes died a fortnight later. The identity of the ghostly highwayman – if indeed all the reports are of the same character – remains unknown.

Postscript: the story of the Huyton Highwayman reminds me of a similar story that was related to me by a man named Stephen who I met after a talk on ghosts at St George's Hall in 2003. In the 1960s, Stephen was, by his own admission, a tearaway, and one day the sixteen-year-old Everton hooligan unscrewed the petrol cap of a car in the city centre and threw a lighted match into it. He was lucky to have escaped with his life, for the car almost immediately exploded into a fireball. A policeman gave chase and during the pursuit, the constable suddenly dived forward and grabbed Stephen's legs, bringing him down. Crowds cheered as the policeman then marched the young pyromaniac to the police station. Stephen was sentenced to a borstal on the outskirts of Merseyside, but managed to escape and go on the run. He met another yob – nineteen-year-old skinhead Mark (wanted in connection with a series of thefts from a warehouse in Widnes) – and the two youths set out for London in a dilapidated Ford Anglia that Mark had stolen from Edge Lane a fortnight before. The London police were soon notified and Mark had a feeling the cops in the capital would be lying in wait, and so he went with his intuition and drove towards the suburbs of north-east London, where the car broke down. Stephen and Mark abandoned the steaming vehicle at around 10pm and headed blindly into what they saw as an ideal cover – Epping Forest.

This ancient forest is the remnant of an extensive 60,000 acre hunting ground, used by the chieftains and kings of Neolithic, Saxon, Norman and Tudor Britain. Although there are roads which enable the motorist, horse rider and cyclist to explore Epping Forest, the ancient woodland is only truly appreciated by the rambler on foot, and the young Liverpudlian city-dwellers soon realised just how big the forest was, and how spooky at night, with owls hooting and foxes and other nocturnal creatures rustling about in the undergrowth. Moonlight streamed into the forest on this frosty night, and Stephen was complaining about how hungry he was as Mark selfishly finished off a packet of cheese and onion crisps. All Stephen had eaten since they entered the forest an hour ago was two digestive biscuits, and his stomach was making loud rumbling sounds which Mark seemed to find funny. Young Stephen was also parched.

All of a sudden, as the two young men approached a glade, their noses caught a whiff of something very appetising – as if someone was cooking in the vicinity. And then they both noticed a tiny silverfish-glimmer of light in the distance. They crept towards the light and came upon a fire with three figures sitting around it. Mark whispered to Stephen that the men were probably tramps, but they were cooking something on a spit, and whatever it was, 'is ours for the taking,' he boasted. Stephen had a bad feeling about the silhouetted men around the fire, and thought he and Mark should go the long way around them and get out of the godforsaken forest and find a shop from which to rob food from. Mark started saying he wasn't afraid of anyone and produced a flick-knife, then slowly walked towards the fire and hid behind a tree which gave him a better view of the 'vagrants'.

But they were not vagrants at all. They were three very odd-looking men wearing clothes that would have been worn perhaps two hundred years ago. One wore a three-cornered hat and a long coat with pale coloured trousers and leather boots to his knees. He sat cross-legged, gazing into the flames over which some skinned animal roasted crackling on a spit. Another man, possibly in his thirties, was lying nearby on some folded garments, and his hair was scraped back and he sported a ponytail. He wore the same type of long coat, trousers and boots as his companion, as well as a white shirt. As he lay on his back, he was fiddling with a long firearm that Stephen and Mark had only seen in films depicting the eighteenth century – a flintlock. The third man wore a tricorn hat with a long black coat, and sat facing the fire with his back to the nervous observers. He had a bottle by his side from which he swigged as the teenagers looked on. About twenty to thirty feet behind the outdated men, three horses stood in the row, tethered to the trees, and the rightmost horse was clearly visible because the moonlight was catching the light-coloured marking – or 'blaze' as it is known – on its nose. This horse seemed to sense the presence of Stephen and Mark, and became restless.

'We'd better go,' Mark suddenly whispered, and Stephen didn't have to be told twice. The two young tearaways turned and began to run, and when they had covered about fifty yards, both heard a gruff voice cry out. Stephen thought this was one of the men shouting: 'Who goes there?'

The youths then heard a loud crack and something whistled between their heads and struck the trunk of a tree in front of them, blowing fragments of bark everywhere. Stephen really picked up speed when he realised he was being shot at and ran off at a tangent, away from Mark. The young outlaws eventually found one another back at the place where they had entered the forest, and they wandered back to civilisation, wondering who the three old-fashioned men had been in Epping Forest.

That night, Stephen and Mark were captured by the police, and when they were in custody, were separately questioned as to where they had been earlier, and to different interviewers, both young men gave an identical account of the three men sitting round the fire. A sergeant later told Stephen that in the eighteenth century, the highwayman Dick Turpin and some fellow criminals had a hideout in Epping Forest. The sergeant said he and several other people had seen the ghosts of various people in the forest over the years. Epping Forest is notorious as a place where many a London murderer has buried his victims, and no doubt there are still many bodies awaiting discovery there.

MIMIC

One pleasant summer evening in August 2010, fifty-two-year-old Howard left his house on Aigburth's Sandhurst Street and walked about a hundred yards to the pillar box on the corner of his street and Bryanston Road. As Howard was posting the letter, he saw old Mrs Graves, who was in her seventies, a former neighbour from Errol Street, which runs parallel to Sandhurst Street.

'Hello there,' said Howard and Mrs Graves smiled and nodded to him, then walked on towards Bryanston Road. Howard thought it odd how that she had not stopped to talk, as she usually did, but then he surmised that she wasn't well or perhaps was in a hurry to get home. As he walked back towards his house, Howard saw Mrs Graves walking towards him, which was, of course, quite impossible, as he had just seen her walking down Bryanston Road, about eighty yards behind him. How on earth then, was the old woman now passing his house? She stopped and said to Howard, 'Isn't it a lovely evening?'

Howard nodded, but was so dumbfounded by the apparent 'transportation', he was stuck for words. Later that evening, around 11.30pm, Howard's partner Sandra came home from the local fish and chip shop, where she worked part-time, and said something that made the hairs on the back of Howard's neck stand on end. 'Hey, do you know if old Mrs Graves has a twin sister?' she asked.

Howard shot her a look of surprise.

Sandra then continued, 'She came into the chippy around half-six and got her usual portion of chips and a carton of curry, and then she left, and about ten seconds after she had gone out the shop, her exact double came up to the front of the chippy and just stood there looking at me through the window.'

Howard then told what he had witnessed earlier in the evening when he had gone to post the letter, and Sandra said: 'You're not just saying this to spook me are you?'

'No, I swear, it was like she'd been teleported from around the corner. It was well weird.'

'That's really creeped me out,' said Sandra, and she hugged him as they sat watching the telly, which had been muted. Sandra then recalled something. 'The Mrs Graves who looked in at me had a brooch in her lapel, with like rubies in, and I don't think the Mrs Graves who came in for the curry and chips had any brooch on.'

'There's got to be a rational explanation,' Howard reasoned, stroking Sandra's head as he recalled what seemed to have been the doppelganger of Mrs Graves by the post office pillar box.

Two days later, Mrs Graves came into the chippy and Sandra asked her if she had an identical twin. She said she didn't and asked Sandra why she had posed such an odd question. 'Oh, I just saw your double the other day, that's all,' Sandra told the pensioner, who simply raised her eyebrows and shrugged, stuck for words.

A few days later Howard and Sandra went into their back parlour after Sunday dinner to watch the new huge plasma TV Howard had set up in there. Sandra then took the curtains down and started to clean the windows. Howard read a book on his Kindle and enjoyed a cigarette as he put his feet up. He had spent a fortune on the new TV and unbelievably there was nothing which really interested him on any of the cable channels at that moment, just gardening programmes, cookery shows, repeats of old films and boring documentaries. After about twenty minutes of reading, Howard happened to look up from his Kindle at the cleaned windows, and through them the backs of the other houses and his own backyard wall, and there, sat upon the wall was Kubrick, the tortoise-shell cat belonging to next door. Kubrick sat there with his usual expressionless face, and his green eyes fixed Howard through the window. Howard read a few more pages, then went to chat to Sandra, who was cleaning up in the kitchen. The couple were talking in the kitchen, in front of the sink, when Sandra also noticed Kubrick – who was now sitting further along the wall, peering through the window at her. She smiled and waved at Kubrick, who knew Sandra well and often slunk in from the backyard when the kitchen door was ajar. Sandra would feed him tiny pieces of boiled ham, which he loved (as long as they were not too big, as he was a fussy eater). Sandra opened the kitchen door and waited. Kubrick came inside and when Sandra took some boiled ham out of the fridge, the cat didn't sit looking up at her as he normally would, but instead went into the back parlour where Howard was now impatiently flipping through the TV channels.

Sandra went into the parlour, and began to talk to Kubrick, uttering the nonsensical phrases and tone of voice some people do when they address cats and babies. 'Aw, he's just a ickle baby isn't he?' when suddenly, she went quiet. Howard looked at his girlfriend because he immediately noticed the abrupt silence. He noticed goosebumps on her forearms and fear in her eyes. 'What's up?' Howard asked, knowing instinctively something was wrong.

'That isn't Kubrick!' Sandra suddenly said, backing away from the cat.

The feline glared at her.

'What do you mean?' Howard said as he muted the television.

'Look at his eyes,' said Sandra.

The cat's eyes were now a very dark blue – ultramarine in fact – and not Kubrick's usual yellowish green. Howard felt a cold shudder when this discrepancy was pointed out to him, and also noticed that the cat seemed longer than the neighbour's cat, and its neck considerably longer.

'Oh, my God, look!' Sandra pointed to the window, and there on the backyard wall, was Kubrick taking swipes at a tiny fly that was too small to be seen by Howard or Sandra.

The couple then turned to look back at the other cat – and its face seemed to have taken on an almost human quality. The cat then scooted into the kitchen, from where it shot off towards the open door. When Sanrda looked into the yard, she saw only the real friendly Kubrick, who came running up to nuzzle against her legs.

Almost an hour went by before Howard said something which made Sandra really stop and think. It was odd how he and Sandra had both seen someone imitating Mrs Graves not so long ago, and now 'something' was impersonating their neighbour's cat. Sandra tried to argue that it was just coincidence. Someone had looked like Mrs Graves, and some cat with the same tortoise-shell markings had come on the scene. But deep down, Sandra felt a deep unease that something supernatural was going on, and Howard definitely believed that this was so. But the biggest shock was yet to come.

Three days later, on the Wednesday of that week, Howard went out with three male colleagues he worked with at a garage off Aigburth Road. Sandra said she'd be okay staying in that night with a few female friends she'd known since her school days. Howard and his mates went on a pub crawl around the city centre and ended up in the Philharmonic on Hope Street, from where they finally all went their separate ways around 11.30pm. As Howard flagged down a cab to take him home to Aigburth, his mobile rang. It was Sandra, asking how his 'blokes night out' had gone. Howard said it had gone okay, but he was now on his way home. He also asked Sandra if she wanted him to stop off anywhere to get her and her mates a kebab or pizza. 'Nah, we're all stuffed, love,' Sandra told him, 'you just get back as soon as you can. I missed you tonight.'

Howard began to feel a little peckish as he rode home in the cab, and so he asked the taxi driver to stop at a kebab house. The cabbie said he knew a really good one nearby, and Howard asked if he wanted anything to eat. The cabbie declined but thanked him anyway. Howard bought his kebab and was soon home – but Sandra wasn't there. He went into the kitchen, and then the back parlour, but she was nowhere to be seen. He went upstairs to the bedroom to find Sandra asleep in bed. When he woke her up she told him that the husband of one of her mates, Jenny, had come round to the house around 9pm in a drunken state, and accused Jenny of cheating on him. He had become so violent, Sandra had called the police and they had taken him away. Jenny then had to be taken home after admitting she had actually had an affair with someone. And so by 9.30pm, Sandra's two other friends had decided to call it a day too and Sandra then went to bed.

'But you called me about half an hour ago,' said Howard.

'No I didn't, I've been in bed since around ten.'

'I asked you if you wanted anything bringing in and you said you were stuffed.'

'Well I'm starving actually,' Sandra told him, looking at the wrapped up kebab carton that was still in Howard's hand. 'Maybe you misdialled and called someone else?'

'No, listen,' said Howard, 'you phoned me ... it was you ...' his voice trailed off as he suddenly recalled the strange incidents concerning Mrs Graves and the neighbour's cat and a chill ran through his body. Sandra guessed exactly what he was thinking. 'What are they playing at?' Howard murmured. 'What's going on?'

'Let's see your phone,' said Sandra, and Howard handed it to her. She navigated through the menu and saw her number time-stamped on the 'calls received' page. When she checked her own mobile, it plainly showed that no calls had been made from that mobile to Howard's mobile since the day before. That morning, at around 4am, Howard awoke to hear Sandra calling him from downstairs. He was about to get up when he realised that she was lying next to him, fast asleep. Still the voice, which was distinctively Sandra's, called out from somewhere downstairs. 'Howard!' shouted the impostor. 'Howard, here!'

Howard woke up Sandra who also heard the familiar voice calling out for Howard. Then, after about five minutes, the voice ceased and an uneasy silence descended on the house, which was suddenly pierced by an eerie sound from outside. A cat began to meow loudly, and suddenly that cat began to call out Howard's name as clear as if a human was reciting it. Howard walked over towards the blinds.

Sandra tried to stop him, 'No! Howard, don't look out! Please, if you love me, don't look out!'

But Howard's curiosity won, and he went to the window and peered out through the gaps in the Venetian blinds. At first he could see nothing, but then, when his eyes had adjusted to that faintly illuminated alleyway below, he saw what looked like the striking pitch-black silhouette of a woman, crouched in an unnatural stance on the top of the backyard wall. Howard swore softly under his breath and Sandra said, 'What? Who is it?'

'Come and have a look, hurry up,' but when Sandra reached the blinds, she only caught sight of a slight movement outside. Howard said the thing had jumped off the wall and had run off down the alleyway. It looked like a woman's outline and yet it moved like an animal – like a cat.

Even when the pale blue light of predawn filtered into the bedroom through the blinds, Sandra still lay awake, listening out for the 'mimic' – something supernatural which she suspected of playing games with her and her boyfriend. The couple finally fell asleep around 6am, and slept through till eleven. They decided that perhaps they should stay away from the house for a few days, and they went to Sandra's parents' house for four days. When they returned to the house on Sandhurst Road, they were naturally very edgy, and feared the mimic would soon be playing its warped games with them once again, but thankfully, Howard and Sandra have had no further strange encounters with the thing which bizarrely seems to have masqueraded as a cat and two humans.

Such supernatural mimics undoubtedly exist, and I clearly remember interviewing a woman who said she went upstairs to her small daughter one day, after hearing her call out her name. When she went into the child's bedroom, the child was sitting on the bed, but facing the wall, and as the mother was about to approach her, she happened to glance through the bedroom window and noticed her 'real' daughter playing outside. Only then did she sense that the thing on the bed was some eerie impersonator of her child, and she turned and ran out the room as the sinister sham child laughed in a deep voice.

I also once interviewed a policewoman named Penny who told me how, when she was twelve, she saw a boy dangling from the branch of a tree sobbing. The tree was in Birkenhead Park, and the boy, Charles, was well known to her. He was five years of age and always seemed to be dressed in a distinctive orange and black striped teeshirt. On this particular afternoon, Charles screamed as he hung from a branch, probably after climbing the tree and losing his nerve. Penny shinned up the tree shouting, 'It's okay, Charlie! I'll get you, hang on!'

But when Penny climbed along the branch and offered her hand to Charles, she saw, to her utmost horror, that the face of the boy was old and wizened, and was fixed in an evil grin. Penny let out a scream and crawled back so quickly along the branch that she lost her footing and fell, winding herself as she landed. She ran off, unable to shout out because she couldn't breathe properly with the impact of the fall. As she ran off through the park, she almost collided with the real Charles, who was, as usual, wearing his distinctive striped teeshirt. Just what the thing was that imitated the little boy remains unknown.

SILHOUETTES

Back in the long-gone summer of 1985, in June to be a bit more precise, a rather shy twenty-year-old called Matthew Wirke decided to go and stay with his Auntie Ruth, a very spiritual and well, let's say a little odd woman, in her late sixties, who seemed to be shunned by her family most of the time. She lived in an old Victorian house close to Sefton Park, on Ullet Road. Her husband Stan had recently died and she had inherited the contents of his bank account – an account he had never shared with his wife while he was alive. Matthew really got on with Ruth, and found her a fascinating person, a born storyteller, and her apple and cinnamon pies were the most delicious things he had ever tasted. Now that Ruth was widowed and alone, Matthew volunteered to stay with her for a while, even though his father, who was Ruth's youngest brother, had warned him against staying with her.

On the first day of his visit, Ruth told him to accompany her in a taxi to Boots in the city centre, where she wanted to buy a newfangled contraption called a microwave oven, which could miraculously cook food in minutes. Matthew eagerly went with her, and for the princely sum of £269.95, Ruth purchased the Russell Hobbs microwave. The man at Boots boasted that this big microwave was 'commodious enough to cook a fifteen-pound turkey' – and so Ruth promptly went out and purchased a turkey of that exact weight to put his claim to the test – and the salesman at Boots had been right. For two days, Ruth and Matthew enjoyed turkey roast and turkey sandwiches, until the third day, when Ruth gave the half-eaten carcass to the foxes of Sefton Park.

On the following day, Matthew woke up in the 'guest bedroom' just after noon. He had gone to bed late the night before and had read a football magazine called *Shoot!* until about 2am, whilst also listening to the radio. There came a rapping on his door, followed by the faint but distinctive voice of his aunt. 'May I come in, Matthew?' she asked.

'Yeah,' Matthew replied, and sat up in the old bed, wondering what this was all about.

Aunt Ruth came into the room carrying a portable television with a loop aerial on the top of it, and the logo on the front had interlocking red green and blue discs – which obviously meant the set was a colour one. Matthew was excited.

'A little something for you,' Ruth said with a lively wink, and she put the new television on the dresser, then said, 'Put it wherever you like, but I think there are only two plug points in here.'

'Ah, you shouldn't have, auntie,' Matthew told her, not meaning a word of it, of course, and he got out the bed in nothing but his maroon Y fronts and went to inspect the television.

On the following day, Matthew went home, but when his father, Terry, saw the colour portable he said, 'You're not having that in this house,' and Matthew and his two older sisters looked at one another with baffled expressions before looking back at their father's reddening face.

'Why not?' Matthew wanted to know.

'Well, if you want that thing in here you can pay the colour telly licence for a start!' said Matthew's father, his eyes bulging.

'Oh, no one will know ...' began Matthew when his father began to shout and bawl.

'Oh and you won't be the one going to prison or getting a big fine if the telly man happens to call here, will you, eh?' he yelled at his son. 'There are thousands of people prosecuted every year and they all thought the telly man would never call on them!'

'You'll have to watch it at your auntie's, Matthew,' said Ada, Matthew's mother, from the doorway of the living room.

'Oh I'd be better off just living with me Auntie Ruth, I would!' Matthew told his father, and stormed out of the room in a huff, almost colliding with his mum in the hallway.

'Go and stay with her then!' Matthew's father shouted after his sulky son, and as Matthew hurried up the stairs to his room clutching his precious television, his dad gripped the stair-rail and shouted: 'Let her pay the bleedin' licence fee!'

'She already does!' Matthew shouted down the stairs, 'She's got a colour telly of her own!'

'Honestly, Dad, we must be the only house in Liverpool that still has a black and white set,' said Tracy, Matthew's twenty-two-year-old sister.

'Well if you could get a proper well-paid job we'd have one wouldn't we?' her father replied, and he put his newspaper under his arm and stormed off through the open kitchen door to the garden. Terry grumpily complained, 'God, this friggin' door's wide open! They've probably heard everything next door. He'll be here tomorrow, just wait and see!'

'Who'll be here, Terry? Who're you talking about?' Ada asked, attempting a grin.

Terry rolled his eyes. 'The telly man, of course! The flippin' telly man! You think it's all a joke with that stupid grin on your face ...'

'You've got this bleedin' bee in your bonnet about the telly man, ever since ...' Ada stopped herself when she realised she was about to say something she was not supposed to divulge.

'Go on! Tell them, you stupid mare!' Terry barked.

'Tell us what?' Pauline, their eldest daughter asked.

'If you must know I got done by the telly man, many years ago, when you two were at school. Nearly got sent down, and it was only a black and white telly!'

'Oh!' said Pauline.

'Tell that to your divvy brother up there,' said Terry prodding his daughter's chest with the end of the rolled up tabloid.

'Alright, alright, Dad, stop overreacting will you?' Pauline pushed the newspaper away, 'You can get telly stamps, it's no big deal! I'll get them if you want!'

'I'll help you get them as well!' Tracy chipped in.

Just then the front door of the house slammed hard. Ada looked through the narrow window at the side of that front door, and through the net curtain she saw Matthew hurrying down the path with his portable in a huge purple hold-all, no doubt bound for Auntie Ruth's.

Auntie Ruth generously offered to pay for a colour television licence to cover Matthew's house, but her nephew shook his head and said, 'Nah, you've done enough, Auntie.'

But of course, Ruth was a very generous woman, and now she had some money behind her, she went out the next day and bought the colour TV licence for Matthew. That evening, Matthew lay on the bed in the guest bedroom of his aunt's home on Ullet Road, thinking about all the arguments he and his sisters were always having with their father. Terry seemed to be getting more grumpy and crotchety as he got older, whereas just five years ago, he would go to the park and play football with Matthew, and would often take the family out to Blackpool and sometimes down to London. As Matthew mused about those happier times, he thought he heard two people – a man and a woman – arguing somewhere close by. He turned down the volume on the portable telly – silence. Matthew had been watching a comedy film

– *Carry On Up the Jungle* – and so he assumed the voices had been from the TV, or perhaps from some interference on the set. In those days, radio transmissions from the police and even taxi radio broadcasts occasionally came through on TV sets. However, later that night, Matthew heard the same voices of the distant couple. He turned down the volume on the television and listened. The voices were still there, and whoever they were they were having a slanging match. Matthew went on to the landing, and listened intently, but now he could hear nothing. He then heard Ruth coming up the stairs on her way to bed. 'Goodnight, Auntie,' Matthew said, and Ruth smiled and replied, 'Night, Matthew. Don't be staying up too late now.'

Matthew went back into his room, and started watching a boring programme called *Database*, which was about personal computers and their use. He changed channels, switching from Granada to catch a quarter of an hour of *Wimbledon 85*, and finding Desmond Lynam's commentary rather soporific, he soon dozed off. When he awoke about half an hour later, Matthew caught the last few minutes of *International Athletics* before the weather forecast came on, followed by the closedown of BBC1. He switched over to BBC2, and seeing it featured nothing but the highlights of the first day's play at Lords between England and Australia, he reluctantly switched off the television, turned off the light, and climbed into bed. Matthew's head had only rested on the pillow for about twenty seconds when he distinctly heard the man and woman arguing again. He sat up, more annoyed than baffled, and looked towards the window. Was the sound of the argument coming from the street? He dragged himself out of bed and went to the window. He parted the lace curtains and saw nothing but Ullet Road, bathed in the usual amber light from the streetlamps. The occasional car rolled past below, and a solitary morose-looking young man walked along with his face to the pavement.

'I'll kill you ...' came the male voice of the bickering couple, and this time it definitely came from behind Matthew. He turned on his bedside lamp, and sat on the edge of his bed. He looked at the portable television, then up the wall at two oval-framed pictures, each about eight or ten inches in length. The pictures featured silhouetted profiles of a man and a woman – just their heads and shoulders. The woman's hair was tied up in a bun, and her profile was very elegant with its cute turned-up nose and thin delicate neck which contrasted with the man's collar length hair and long aquiline nose. The two silhouettes were positioned six inches apart, facing each other, so as to make them appear to be looking at each other.

As Matthew Wirke looked at the framed silhouettes, he noticed something that immediately made him think he might be dreaming. The man's head was clearly moving; its lips faintly opening and closing, and he was moving his head backwards and forwards slightly as he talked. The same eerie phenomenon was evident in the female silhouette, only her mouth was opening much wider as if she was shouting something.

Matthew slowly rose from his bed with his heart pounding in his chest. The voices from the animated pictures were growing in intensity: 'Needles and pins, needles and pins, when a young man marries his trouble begins!' shouted the male silhouette.

'I should never have married you!' screamed the woman. Her shrill voice sounded young, maybe just out of her teens.

'Eve, I will have none of your rotten apple!' the man bawled.

'Matthew! Can you turn the telly down please?' Aunt Ruth's voice came through the bedroom wall. She had heard the quarrelling pair from next door; that's how loud they sounded.

Matthew was about to shout back that it wasn't the television that was making the racket, but before he could open his mouth, the male silhouette reached out of the oval frame with two long black spindly arms, and the wiry-looking hands seized the little neck of the silhouetted woman and began to throttle her. The shadow man shook her head vigorously and the woman's mouth opened wide as she was steadily throttled.

'Needles and pins, needles and pins, when a young man is married his trouble begins!' yelled the sinister two-dimensional strangler, and he shook his victim in the other frame with such force, her bun became undone. She uttered a ghastly rasping sound, and her head became limp in the crushing, strangling hands of her killer. Matthew ran out of the room and flew along the landing towards his Auntie Ruth's door. He banged hard and then barged in to see his aunt getting out of bed in her nightie. 'Matthew! I told you to turn the sound down!' she sternly told her nephew.

'It isn't the telly, Auntie Ruth, please come and see!' And Matthew beckoned her out on to the dark landing, and Ruth followed him. 'You won't believe this!' he shouted, and led her into his bedroom, where she witnessed the same terrifying spectacle.

'Oh God!' Ruth clutched Matthew's upper arm. She then dragged him from the room as he looked back in horror as the silhouetted strangler shook his floppy-headed victim who was now as limp as a rag doll. As aunt and nephew went down the stairs, they could both hear the faint but gleeful words coming from the guest bedroom: 'Needles and pins, needles and pins ...'

Ruth and Matthew stood in the kitchen in a terrible state. Ruth was shaking and Matthew was trying to pretend he wasn't scared but the look of fear was clearly in his eyes. 'Maybe I should go and stay over with your father,' Ruth suggested, but she wondered how she'd be able to muster enough courage to go back upstairs to get her clothes from her wardrobe.

'He was strangling her!' Matthew murmured, and now his fear was giving way to confusion. 'Whose silhouettes are they, Auntie?'

'They belonged to my husband Stan ... I think they were the actual silhouettes of his grandparents. It's so strange.'

They heard movement on the stairs, and both froze. Ruth went to the kitchen door and looked out across the half-lit hallway – and recoiled in shock.

'What is it, Auntie?' Matthew, asked, and then he crept to the doorway and peered over his aunt's shoulder. For a few moments he could not make out what she was staring at – and then he saw it. On the top step of the bottom flight of stairs leading to the ground floor was a pair of jet-black legs, visible only from the knees to the shoes.

'Needles and pins, needles and pins ...' came that voice again from the stairs, and those spindly legs began to descend the stairs ever so slowly. Ruth and Matthew ran across the hallway and Ruth screamed as she heard footsteps closing in on herself and her nephew. She undid the catch on the Yale lock, opened the door and she and Matthew stumbled outside. Matthew looked back, and then slammed the front door shut with one powerful pull. He and Ruth then walked in a daze in their night clothes along Ullet Road, where Ruth flagged down a taxi. She and her nephew rode the cab to Matthew's home in Edge Hill. Just before the taxi reached his house, Ruth asked her nephew what he had seen when he looked back into the hallway just before he slammed the door. Matthew said he had seen the flat-looking shadow of a man, but that walking silhouette had a pair of evil-looking blue eyes which had glared at him.

Ruth's brother Terry dismissed the story about the haunted pictures as hysterical twaddle, and went over to Ruth's house in the morning to get her clothes. Luckily for Ruth, Terry had kept a spare set of her house keys for a few years. Terry took a look in the guest room and found the supposedly haunted silhouettes on the wall. He could see nothing untoward about them, and he decided to bring them over to his house. 'Are these the so-called haunted pictures then?' he asked, looking pointedly at Ruth and Matthew in turn, and he took the oval framed silhouettes from a burlap bag and plonked them down on the dining room table.

Ruth recoiled in horror and asked her brother how he could be so insensitive as to bring over the very objects that had struck fear into the hearts of both her and Matthew. She seized the portraits and went into the back garden to hurl them into the bin.

By 4pm that day, Ruth decided she'd go back home, and Matthew accompanied her.

On the following morning at 11am, there was a frantic knocking at the door of Ruth's Ullet Road house. Ruth answered to find her two nieces – Matthew's sisters Tracy and Pauline – both as pale as death. Before they had even set foot in the house they began to babble about strange goings-on at their house, and Ruth ushered them into the kitchen and sat them down with a cup of tea and some biscuits and then told them to start again from the beginning – slowly.

Matthew, always the late riser, was coming down the stairs, and heard the familiar voices in the kitchen. He said hello to his sisters but they were too busy talking over one another as they related the strange events of the previous night. Tracy had heard a couple arguing and screaming at around half-past eleven. Then around half-past one in the morning, they had heard terrible screams from the back garden, and Pauline had gone into the upstairs toilet to open the window, which looked on to the garden – and she had seen the silhouettes of a man and a woman, dressed in old fashioned clothes, striking one another. Pauline went and fetched Tracy, who also saw them. The girls went to tell their father, who was already getting up because he had also heard the arguers and was going to give them a piece of his mind. Leaning out of the toilet window he saw the couple fighting, but could only make them out as shadows with no features; like animated life-size figures cut out of black card. Instantly he recalled what Ruth and Matthew had told him about the strange silhouettes – and then, with a shiver, he remembered that Ruth had thrown those framed silhouettes into the bin in the back garden.

Terry shut the window and ordered his daughters back to bed. They asked if he was going to tell the couple to shut up so everyone could sleep but Terry just ignored his daughters' questions and went back to bed himself. The next morning Terry and the rest of the family were relieved when the binmen turned up and emptied the bin containing the accursed oval portraits into the refuse wagon.

After that day, Ruth was never troubled by the silhouettes again, and there were no further paranormal goings-on at Matthew's house in Edge Hill.

Ruth sadly passed away in the early 1990s, but Matthew asked me to research her husband's grandparents to see if I could possibly throw any light on the haunted picture frames. I discovered a few things that Matthew preferred me not to publish, but he would allow me to print the following. Stan's grandfather most probably strangled his first wife, Eve, in the early 1870s in Liverpool, but claimed it was a cousin who was later tried and saved from the noose because he was believed to be already suffering from a form of insanity before the alleged murder took place.

A few years later, in the summer of 1875, Stan's grandfather was living in the Walton area of Liverpool with his second wife, whom he also attacked on several occasions, and in June of that year, he was briefly interviewed by police after the body of thirteen-year-old Edward Howell was found hidden beneath shrubbery and brushwood in Anfield Cemetery. The boy had been strangled elsewhere and dumped in the cemetery by his murderer. At the time, Stan's grandfather was seeing a woman who lived in Bidston View, off Walton Road, in Kirkdale; the very same street where a widow named Margaret Howell – the mother of the dead boy – had lived. The murderer of Edward Howell was never brought to justice, despite a reward being offered, and there were other strange murders in that part of Liverpool in the years after the 1875 strangling case – and Stan's grandfather was always living within a stone's throw of each murder scene.

When Matthew was presented with all of this evidence he was deeply shocked, to say the least, and asked me to refrain from naming his distant ancestor. I assured him I would use false names in the story, and told him that most families would uncover a skeleton or two in their cupboard if they dug deep enough through the generations into the murky past. I cannot explain the phenomenon regarding the silhouettes, and wonder if they now lie in some landfill site in south Liverpool – or whether some curious binman in the 1980s spotted them in that bin and took them home ...

A Grim Premonition

Unless you have a strong stomach, you might do well to skip this chapter.

In May 1846, fifty-year-old Margaret Davies moved from her Liverpool home to Ireland to live in Collooney, County Sligo, with her husband George, a fisherman who had been born in that county fifty-five years before. Margaret hadn't settled down long in her little cottage with George when she began to be plagued by a series of terrifying, vivid dreams in which she was subjected to the most gruesome sights. All the dreams involved some violent tragedy that unfolded on a ship, and were so graphic, Margaret would sometimes throw up after waking from the grisly nightmares. George feared for his wife's mental health and was about to seek the advice of the parish priest when the dreams thankfully stopped. But then something strange and disturbing took place.

George's niece, Mary, who lived about twenty miles away from them in Sligo, wrote to George to tell him how she and her husband and baby son were about to go to Liverpool to make a new life for themselves. George read how Mary and her husband and baby were due to board a new steam ship called *The Rambler* the following Saturday. Straight away, Margaret Davies told George that one of the ships in her nightmare had been called *The Rambler* and she urged George to visit his niece to talk her out of going, but George put his wife's weird dreams down to indigestion, of eating before bed, something which Margaret was fond of doing.

And so Mary boarded *The Rambler* with her husband and child, and that vessel, commanded by one Captain McCallister, left Sligo on Saturday, 23 May 1846, and headed out into the waters of Donegal Bay, bound for Liverpool. Because of a technical problem involving a shortage of water for the ship's steam engine, *The Rambler* was forced to drop anchor until the problem was addressed, and the delay resulted in the vessel raising anchor on the Sunday afternoon. She resumed her journey to Liverpool heavily laden; in addition to her goods cargo, *The Rambler* was carrying seven hundred pigs and twenty head of cattle, and the shortage of room on board the ship forced the stevedores to put some of the animals on deck. There were also around four hundred and fifty men, women and children onboard the steamer, as well as the crew, of course, and the stench below decks was almost unbearable throughout the passage from Sligo.

By Monday night, at 10.45pm, *The Rambler* had reached the mouth of the Mersey, and as she passed the Perch Rock Lighthouse off New

Brighton, the steamer's captain looked in horror at another ship coming towards it. The ship on a collision course with *The Rambler* was the *Sea Nymph*, which had just left Liverpool's Clarence Dock, bound for Cork, commanded by Captain Joseph Thomson. This ship was also packed to the gunnels with passengers. The helms of the two ships were rapidly spun to port, but to no avail, and witnesses on both sides of the river described a sound like a loud clap of thunder when *The Rambler* and the *Sea Nymph* impacted, followed by the agonised stomach-churning screams and wails of the passengers – as well as the squeals and shrieks of pigs and cattle – coming from both ships.

The pointed bow of the *Sea Nymph* had rammed into the bows of *The Rambler*, cutting the inward-bound vessel in two as far as the waterline, severing the deck halfway across and shaking its entire frame, rendering each of its water-tight compartments perfectly useless.

So much for the damage to the material fabric of the ship, but what of the gruesome toll on the human passengers and animal cargo both on deck and in the hold? Consider that the bow of the vessel – the point of cataclysmic impact – was packed with men, women and children, as well as pigs and cattle. The victims who had not been horrifically mutilated and injured by the collision stampeded in panic like the animals among them, and many people were trampled to death, including one poor woman who was seen almost naked on the deck, a bloody flattened mess of crushed skull and broken bones, trampled by human and animal feet as the ship started to sink and a terrible frenzy spread amongst all on board. Another trampled victim, a young girl, had her mouth open wide, and her front teeth embedded in the wooden boards of the deck, and the pressure upon her had popped out one of her eyes and burst her tiny torso.

Over a dozen passengers jumped into one of the lifeboats, and instead of waiting for one of the crew to lower the boat into the sea, someone cut the ropes in panic and the lifeboat fell, capsised, and everyone on board was drowned. Mary Connolly, who survived the tragedy, told newspaper reporters in the Northern Hospital (where she made a remarkable recovery) how she saw one of her children kneeling with clasped hands as if in prayer when she came round after the collision, but when she tried to grab at him, his arm came out of the socket of his shoulder, and she realised he was dead. Mary tried to rescue another child among the carnage and saw his entire face come away with a gush of blood. One passenger stripped naked and jumped off *The Rambler*, intending to swim to the Wirral shore, but the current pulled him under, and he would have drowned if he hadn't been saved by a boy and a fireman who dived in after him from the sinking ship.

Blue signal rockets were fired from *The Rambler* to alert the Magazine lifeboat, and many heroic rescues took place that traumatic night. Fifty to sixty souls were picked up by the Magazine lifeboat on the first trip, but on the second return trip, to the bows of *The Rambler*, the rescue team saw the most sickening sights that would haunt them for the rest of their lives. The wreckage was drenched with mingled human and animal blood, and the most heart rending spectacles met their eyes. A little boy gazed at the rescuers with a look of bewildered terror on his face, and his body below the navel was described as 'crushed mincemeat'. The child whimpered then passed away in the arms of one sobbing rescuer. The lifeboatmen then came upon a woman whose legs were pinned down by an iron beam, and the bones of the mangled legs were horrifically broken and crushed to a pulp by the ankles. They did all they could to rescue her from the tangled mass of twisted metal frames and splintered wood. With her face contorted in agony, the unfortunate young woman cried: 'I have four pounds in my pocket, and if you'll get me out I'll give you all that! Please get me out!' By some miracle, as the ship went steadily down, the rescuers managed to free the woman, who looked down at the gruesome remains of what were once her shapely legs, now dangling from her kneecaps.

Below this woman, the lifeboatmen came upon a dead mother in her twenties, with her crushed baby still in her arms, and the dead infant's mouth was still at its mother's breast. Two of the boatmen, accustomed to some of the most gruesome aspects of shipwreck and disaster, began to cry silently at the sight of the dead mother and child.

A boat called the *Elizabeth*, moored over by the Perch Rock lighthouse, soon arrived to rescue more of the victims from both ships. Hundreds were saved as a result. The Reverend Lennon of Liscard was sent for, and he was soon administering spiritual consolation to the survivors, many of whom had sustained terrible injuries. Many Wirral people opened their doors to the victims on that terrible night, and gave them food, beds and of course, human kindness. Several little boys, who had become separated from their parents in the tragic collision, were welcomed into a house by a Miss Waistell, and one of these children, two-year-old boy Paddy Connolly, was thought to be an orphan, as no one claimed him for weeks, but he was later reunited with his parents, who had been recovering from severe injuries at the Northern Hospital in Liverpool. Unfortunately, Paddy's brothers and sisters had perished in the accident. No one ever came to claim another little boy who had been put in the care of Miss Waistell, so she adopted him as one of her own.

The remains of thirteen dead bodies, shipped from *The Rambler*, were placed in the Magazine lifeboat house, pending identification, and presented a most ghastly sight to those who came to view them. It has to be said that many came to look at them out of plain morbid curiosity. The maimed, fractured and mutilated bodies lay there, side by side. Thirteen individuals who, only a matter of hours before, had been in the full possession of life, vigour and enthusiasm, many of them looking forward to landing at Liverpool. Now they were the blackened remains of mothers, fathers, brothers, sisters, most of them covered in gore. Some had obviously died an agonising death, by the looks of their clenched teeth, clenched fists, and twisted faces. The arm of a child was laid next to his little body; at his side a man in his thirties with his foot torn off. The body of a seven-year-old child lay without a face, and on closer inspection, that missing face was to be seen lying folded next to his head like the skin of a cooked chicken. The woman next to him was mangled like a broken doll.

When a police superintendent examined the pockets of the dead, not a single coin was found in any of them. The wreckage of *The Rambler*, which remained buoyant, was towed across the river and eventually repaired at the Clarence Dock, as was the *Sea Nymph*. It was later discovered that the captain and mate of the *Sea Nymph* had 'been in liquor' before the ship set out for Cork.

Over in Collooney, Sligo, the Liverpool woman Margaret Davies almost fainted when the news of the terrible collision reached her ears. She had dreamt of the tragedy in appalling detail, and unfortunately, Mary, the niece of Margaret and George who had boarded *The Rambler*, perished in the disaster. 'Oh why didn't I heed you?' Margaret's husband wailed, 'and now we've lost our darling girl'. As far as I know, Margaret Davies had no further premonitions after that day.

THE TROJAN SOFA

This very strange story unfolded many years ago in the late 1970s. Around July 1979, Kevin, a fourteen-year-old house-robber, bumped into a thirteen-year-old scallywag named Chris. They met whilst robbing the same youth club somewhere in south Liverpool, each unaware of the other's existence until they collided in the club's kitchen, where they ransacked the fridge, removing blocks of ice cream and cans of soft drink. That night, they removed the record player and hi-fi system, loudspeakers, amplifier and microphones, a classical guitar, and a little metal box containing money collected by the students who ran the club for the hire of a coach to take local underprivileged kids to Blackpool. That money was squandered in the video-game arcades on Lime Street, as were the proceeds accrued from the sale of the stolen items to fences.

Then one day, Kevin and Chris visited a second-hand furniture store to see if there was anything they could rob, but most of the items were simply too big to run off with. This second-hand store was housed in a disused church, and the elderly man who ran it was very trusting. He never dreamt the angel-faced teens roaming the store were opportunistic criminals. Chris suddenly hit on an idea. 'Hey, you know what we could do?' he asked Kevin in an excited tone. 'I've got a cracker idea, listen.'

And Chris told Kevin his idea in a careful whisper close to his ear, 'I could use my Stanley knife to slit that sofa open over there, under the cushions like, along like a seam, and then get in it, and then just lie there. And when the arl fellah locks up this place I'll come out the sofa and unlock the door.'

Kevin thought about the crazy proposition. 'Yeah, but he locks the place up with a padlock, so how can you let me in?'

'No, there's a door he goes out of over there, look,' Chris whispered, nodding to the doorway at the side of the church. And he was right, it was a reinforced door, with only a simple Yale lock. Outside, there was only one way to open it – with a Yale key, but inside, all Chris would have to do was turn the brass knob to let his friend in.

'Go 'ead then,' Kevin said, with a rasping laugh. 'I'll keep dixie.'

'Unless you wanna do it?' Chris offered, looking a little flushed in his face.

Kevin shook his head vigorously. 'No, you do it; you suggested it, go 'ead!'

'It's too early yet, he doesn't lock up till five, and its only twenty-five to,' Chris replied, eyeing the old grandfather clock that had a sign on it saying 'Not for Sale'.

Kevin had a suggestion. 'Lets go and have a look at the sofa first and make sure we can cut an opening in it where you could be skied away.'

As luck would have it, the old man's attention was drawn to an old woman who doddered into the premises on a zimmer frame. She asked him if he had any old sideboards. 'Yes, the sideboards are over here, madam,' said the well-spoken old man, and he led his aged customer to the other side of the cold room.

The young crooks hurried to the huge sofa – which bore a large SOLD sign upon it – and began to remove the four cushions. It felt a bit hollow and saggy anyway. Chris got his Stanley knife out and quickly created a long slit about four feet in length in the material, then began to scoop out some brown straw-like stuffing. Chris swore as he pushed a few old springs back inside and then said to Kevin, 'You're smaller than me; you'd easily fit in there.'

'Not likely, it's your idea.'

Both lads kept taking turns to look over at the old man who was just visible through the clutter of furniture. Chairs on tables, floor lampstands, bureaux, chests of drawers, wardrobes, Welsh dressers, and assorted junk all conspired to give excellent cover to the two young scoundrels as they created the Trojan Sofa. All of the stuffing removed from the sofa was placed in the drawers of nearby cabinets and sideboards, and then, just before the old woman on the zimmer frame, having rejected all the sideboards, left the furniture store empty handed, Chris wriggled into the hollow of the sofa and Kevin sniggered as he covered him up with the lining fabric before placing the four cushions on top of him.

'What are you doing over there?' the old man peeped from behind a mahogany breakfront bookcase.

'Nothin', just lookin' at the sofa, mate,' Kevin replied.

'Well. I'm closing in a minute,' said the old man, then vanished back among the jumble of furniture.

Kevin left the old church and walked to a local shop, where he stole a few packets of sweets. When he came out, there was a crimson transit van parked outside the church, and a white curly-haired man and a much younger man, were carrying that sofa out of the church and walking towards the van.

Kevin went cold. He had to do something to distract the men so that Chris could escape from the sofa. So he shouted to the older one, 'Hey, mate! Some kid's letting your front tyres down!'

The older man halted for a moment, then stretched his neck out and looked around the open back doors of the transit van. 'Where? I can't see anyone.'

'There! He's letting them down!' said Kevin, pointing at the van's front right tyre.

The old man swore and said, 'Go on, beat it!'

And the men lifted the sofa into the van and slammed the doors shut. Kevin wondered whether he should try and open the doors and get poor Chris out of there – but decided it wasn't worth the risk. It'd be too bad if Chris was caught, but Kevin didn't think his 'oppo' was worth getting into trouble for, and so he walked off, munching the Star Bar he had stolen.

Chris, meanwhile, crouched inside his claustrophobic hole, listening to the transit van's engine rev into life. He felt the van move off, and wondered whether anyone was standing by the sofa in the back of the van. He wanted to peep out from behind the cushions but was scared in case someone saw him. He lay there in the sweltering heat, cursing Kevin for not carrying out this job. The van started to accelerate and swerved as it rounded a corner, and then, just when Chris decided he'd have to get out of the sofa, the van came to a halt. It had arrived at its destination by the sounds of it, as the engine had stopped.

The sounds of the van doors being opened could be clearly heard, and then Chris felt the sensation of the two men jumping into the van. The floor shook. Boots thumped closer.

'Shall I take the cushions off or carry it with them on?' asked a rough voice.

Oh, please leave them on! Chris thought.

'Nah, leave 'em, you get the other end and back out,' said the older, deeper voice.

The sofa rocked unsteadily as the men's four hands grappled with it. 'This weighs a bleedin' ton,' complained the younger voice. 'Sure there's no murder victim stuck in here?'

'You're out of shape, lad,' said the other, 'I could hear you wheezing before when we got it into the van.'

'Wheezing?'

'Yeah, first sign you're out of shape.'

And the men carried the long sofa into the house and placed it down somewhere. A man with an effeminate-sounding voice could then be heard, saying: 'Ah, thanks, boys. Wait there, I have a little something for you,' and Chris heard him patter away. In his absence, the younger man said, 'He sounds like a pufter. He's dead tall as well, ain't he?'

'Hey, shut up, he's alright him. A bit eccentric, like, but he's alright. Just talks funny, yeah, and he is a bit too tall; get your ball off the roof though.'

The gentle tapping of feet returned, and the camp-sounding man said, 'There's your money and here's a cake I baked just for the two of you.'

'Ah, you shouldn't have bothered, Mr Kearns,' said the older-sounding voice.

The two van drivers left, and then Mr Kearns began to sing a song that had been in the charts a few years before; *Seasons in the Sun* by Terry Jacks. And then he must have sat down on the sofa, because Chris felt the cushion above press down hard on his face, and for a few moments he could hardly breath in the suffocating confines of the sofa, but, just before the teenager could attempt to push upwards at the smothering cushion, Mr Kearns got his backside off the sofa to answer a ringing telephone. Enough was enough. Chris felt his right-front jean pocket for the Stanley knife, and cut a small piece out of the back of the sofa to create a peephole. He saw nothing but blue and silver patterned wallpaper about five inches away from his face. He guessed he was in the hallway of the house, and thought he could perhaps just leap out of the sofa and get out of the house as quickly as possible. If Mr Kearns tried to stop him, Chris would have to use the knife on him. He listened first: 'Okay, well I tell you what then, I'll go and collect it now if that's okay. Yes. See you in a mo.'

The telephone receiver could be heard being placed back in its cradle, then Chris heard Kearns singing that Terry Jacks song again. About two minutes later, the front door slammed shut, followed by the sound of keys rattling about in locks. Then Chris could make out the distant thuds of what sounded like Kearns walking away from the house down his garden path. At last he could get out of the accursed sofa and get down to business – robbing a few things from the house before making his getaway. Chris ripped back the coarse jute lining fabric, and then pushed the cushions off him. He sat up and took some long deep breaths. The bright sunlight flooding through the window in the front door stung his eyes after lying in the dark for what seemed like a very long time. He got up off the sofa and had a look about.

He was in the long hallway of a house. What if there was someone else in the place? Chris peeped around the doorway of a parlour. No one was about, not even a pet to be seen. Where should he start? Chris rifled through the kitchen cupboards as fast as he could. Nothing of any value. He went into the living room and in the drawer of a sideboard discovered a biscuit tin containing various documents: a pale blue rent book, a driving licence, an old car tax disc, then bingo! two rolls of ten pound notes that came to £210, bound with elastic bands, as well as a little plastic Barclays bank coin bag full of fifty-pence pieces. 'Very, very nice,' Chris found himself whispering gleefully. He wasn't sure whether he should go upstairs now and have another root, but that might just be pushing his luck. So pocketing the lovely two-hundred-odd quid he decided to make a clean away before Kearns got back.

He went to the kitchen door leading to the backyard, and saw something strange. There was a keyhole about five inches from the floor, and another about five inches from the top of the door. This meant to get out you'd have to unlock the top and then the bottom lock – if you could find the keys, that is – and there were no keys to be found. And so, reluctantly, Chris hurried out of the living room and down the hallway, past the sofa and its scattered cushions – and there he found the same set-up. A lock at the bottom of the door and another at the top. 'What the hell …' Chris complained, and looked about desperately for the keys, for the door had been locked by Kearns before he had set off on his journey. Chris swore under his breath and went back to the kitchen. There, on the wall, was a funny little plaque, about eight inches wide and four inches tall, and the four words on it read: 'We'll watch your keys.' Above it were two little comical models of women in headscarves leaning over a fence with cigarettes in their mouths.

Chris snatched the two separate keys from the hooks on the

plaque and went to the kitchen. He inserted one of the keys into the bottom keyhole and turned it. It clicked. He then tried to open the door. It wouldn't budge. He pulled a chair out from under the kitchen table. It had a spindle-filled backing and a seat made of intertwined rushes. It looked very old – antique even. Christ scraped the legs of the chair across the tiled floor to the door which led to the backyard. He stood on the chair and inserted one of the keys into the keyhole at the top of the door. It turned and clicked. 'Very nice!' our young robber said with satisfaction, and stepped down from the chair. He turned the handle, but the damned door refused to open. 'How the hell are you supposed to open the flamin' thing?' he muttered to himself. It was as if the keys had to be inserted simultaneously into the top and bottom keyholes and turned at the same time, but to do that, Chris's arms would have had to be freakishly long. He took the chair to the front door and tried inserting the key in the top lock. It turned and something clicked, but still the door wouldn't open. He tried the other key in the bottom keyhole and it turned just as easily, but still the door refused to budge. Looking through the frosted half-moon window of the front door, Chris heard the gate handle being pressed. He heard the hinge of the gate squeak as it was pushed open and then closed – and the footfalls. He picked up the chair and ran down the hallway with it to place it under the kitchen table. Chris looked back down the hallway and heard the locks clicking on the front door. He ran to the heavy thick purple curtains that went right down to the floor in the living room and hid behind them.

Moments later he heard Kearns come into the hallway. The front door was still open, and remained open for a while because Chris could hear an ice cream van's jingling theme tune somewhere nearby and the white-noise rush of traffic passing by. The teenaged housebreaker guessed that Kearns was looking at the scattered sofa cushions in the hallway and the ripped fabric. He'd probably already found the hollow Chris had excavated in the back of the sofa. Now was the time to run out from behind the curtains, down the hallway and out of the house – but Kearns slammed the door shut. He didn't come into the living room; he went upstairs. Chris heard his thump-thump-thump on the carpeted stairway. Was he going to call the police? But Chris had not noticed a telephone up there, and it wasn't like him to miss much. The only telephone was on that crescent table in the hallway. Why then, had Kearns gone upstairs? Chris decided that his only option was to smash one of the windows and then just make a break out of the house that way. He hated glass though, because he had slashed his wrist breaking into a house via a window when he was just ten, and had lost so much blood he needed a blood transfusion.

Time dragged on. Chris took the Stanley knife out of his pocket and slid the triangular blade out of the black sleek body. He peeped out from behind the curtain, and at first didn't see Kearns, because clouds had slid over the sun now, making the room gloomy. Suddenly, Chris saw something that literally put the fear of God into him. A man, at least seven feet in height, with abnormally long arms and freakishly long narrow legs, sat facing him in an armchair and on his head he wore a black mantilla veil, of the type a widow might wear at a funeral. He also wore a black blouse of some sort, and a short matte black skirt and black tights. His pointed black shiny shoes were huge, size fourteen at least. He was sitting there with his legs obscenely wide apart so Chris could see the man's black knickers. And in his left hand, this freak of nature held a long carving knife with the blade tip pointing to the ceiling and its black handle resting on the vinyl padded arm of the chair. The eerie transvestite had a deathly pale face with heavy black make-up encircling each eye, and those eyes were fixed on Chris, and seemed full of mockery. The lips were coated with dark red lipstick and curved up in a ghastly grin of discoloured teeth.

'Hello,' the figure said, and Chris immediately recognised the camp tone of the voice. It was indeed Mr Kearns. 'I'm going to cut you up into little bits and I'm going to put you in a pie with some cranberry sauce,' he said.

Chris felt faint. He suddenly remembered the Stanley knife and held it up in a threatening manner, but Kearns just let out a shriek of laughter, and said, 'That doesn't scare me, laddie! Look!' and he lifted up his long thin hand and pressed the tip of the massive carving knife into the centre of his palm, drawing blood. 'Doesn't even hurt! Ha! Ha!'

Chris found himself trying to run past this terrifying figure, but his legs seemed to be moving in slow motion. Kearns was up in a flash and had to duck as he passed through the doorway into the hallway. Chris knew he couldn't get out of the house through that double-locked front door, so he ran up the stairs and into one of the rooms, and when he looked back, he saw the 'woman' in black lumbering awkwardly up the stairs, impeded by his huge long feet, which were too big to take each step on the staircase. 'You won't get away! You're going to be dead meat soon!' he shouted after Chris. Chris pushed open the door to one of the rooms then slammed it shut; a room whose walls were plastered with various female models of the day, and someone had scribbled zig-zag lines on every face with a red marker. There was a white plaster bust of some woman on a sideboard, and her nose had been hacked off. Chris picked up the bust and hurled it at the window, smashing the pane in completely. He looked out of the window and saw the top of the backyard wall about fifteen feet below. He had no choice but to jump out on to it, and fast, even if it meant risking a broken neck. He turned and saw the door of the room open, and the sinister veiled head of the giant psychopath peeped in. 'Come back and I promise you I won't lay a finger on you!' Kearns now promised unconvincingly.

Chris swore at him at the top of his voice, and Kearns let out a spine-chilling scream and rushed into the room. The hand that held the carving knife was raised and ready to strike. Chris stepped on to the bottom of the window frame, crouched, and flung himself out, intending to land on the top of the wall, which he did, but the thick layer of moss that coated the bricks caused him to slip and fall into the entry. He landed on his feet with such a force, he felt as if the tops of his legs had gone through to his chest, and he found himself staggering down the entry, unable to breathe in or out, or utter a single word. He finally emerged from the entry near Aigburth Road and from there he walked the three miles home expecting a knife in his back every step of the way.

Chris suffered realistic recurring nightmares about the weird knife-wielding transvestite for many many years afterwards, until his death in 1986.

More Liverpool Timeslips

I have covered the concept of timewarps and slippages in time in many of my books and it was I who first mentioned the Bold Street timeslips which are now even mentioned on Wikipedia and other internet websites, although some web 'authors' maintain that these incidents are all 'urban myths' (and these nameless, faceless individuals ignorantly insult the integrity and bravery of the many people from all walks of life who come forward to tell me of their experiences). My numerous accounts of the Bold Street timewarps were presented to the public in the hope that other people who had experienced time loss or displacement would come forward to describe what had happened to them, and I was not disappointed. I estimate that well in excess of four hundred people have written to me, or called me at radio stations, to tell me of their timeslip experiences, and rarely a week goes by without a reader contacting me to tell me of yet another timewarp incident which happened to them or someone they know. What follows is just a small selection of these fascinating timeslip accounts.

In the 1960s, a reader named Cathy, who was nineteen when the following incident happened, was a typical teen who loved clothes, and, well, I'll let Cathy tell the story:

It was the Swinging Sixties and I loved buying clothes and wore a wild array of coloured dresses and mini skirts, mostly in clashing colours like orange and pink and purple, usually with boots up to the knees or chunky-heeled shoes. To fund my wardrobe I worked in the city. Jobs were easy to find then, you would give up one job on a Friday, and find another by the following Monday. I went to work for a firm of

119

Chartered Accountants called Charles E Dolby who had offices in old chambers in Dale Street. This was an ancient decrepit building which would have been perfect for a film set of a Dickens drama. I guess nothing had changed since the eighteenth century. A few other businesses occupied the building. I worked on the ground floor in a tiny office with two other girls. About six articled clerks had the next office, and they were paid buttons because they were training to be accountants, but actually did most of the work. The office toilets were located on the top floor, up four flights of stairs and were housed inside a very large room; a room that was definitely not originally made with toilet facilities in mind; it was all such a waste of space, especially as most of the offices were tiny pokey little rooms. This huge room at the top of the building had about eight toilets in cubicles in a line opposite the only door. The toilets were on a higher level, you had to climb up a step. The whole floor area was old wooden boards, not polished but in a dry dusty untreated condition.

All the offices had their own key to this room and the old fashioned door was of very heavy solid oak, with a new Yale lock fitted so when you closed it, it locked behind you. Outside, the steps leading up to this door were made of concrete, obviously a later addition to the building. Now, I've been in many haunted places such as Dean Hall, supposedly the most haunted house in England, and many old pubs and halls with ghosts, and I have never felt a thing – not the slightest vibe, so it is really amazing that whenever I entered this room at the top of the offices I could feel an atmosphere immediately, so much so that I would only use the toilets if I was absolutely desperate. The minute I entered there was a total quietness, it was freezing, I could feel I was being watched. It was absolutely, terrifyingly scary. I never mentioned this to anyone. I don't know why, perhaps they would think me odd. No-one else seemed to be bothered about it and all the staff used the toilets whenever they needed to with no comment.

One morning I decided to get in early, I had stacks of work to do, all the end of year accounts had to be typed and I wanted to get a head start, so I caught an earlier train from my home in Rock Ferry to

James Street Station. I picked up the mail on the way into the building and instead of opening up our office, I needed the loo so without thinking, got the key off the hook in the outer office and ran up all the flights of stairs, opened the big old door and dropping the mail on to a sink went into our office's loo. As soon as I locked the door, the whole room erupted into bedlam. I went into a state of total shock, and was so petrified I couldn't move a muscle. The room outside my cubicle was filled with the sound of wooden clogs running and jumping on the bare boarded floor. Outside the room, the floor and stairs were concrete, so this was all happening inside on the wooden floorboards. Voices – raised and high pitched – were making sounds so terrible I felt if I opened the door I would be faced with mad lunatics all in an uncontrollable frenzy. This went on for ages – and I really mean ages. I stood behind that door unable to move for fifteen to twenty minutes, and all the while pandemonium was on the other side of a thin wooden door with gaps above and below. Even as I recall this my heart is racing; I have never known fear like it.

Somehow I managed to get my brain to work. I realised I had to get out of there; I had to pluck up the courage to make a run for it, through a crowd of crazed ghosts. How do you get up the courage to do that? I was well aware that whatever was making all that noise was not of this earth. They were not human. They were spirits of some sort and definitely not friendly. Even to this day the memory of this is so sharp I will never forget it. I planned to open the door and run, and after a few false starts and shaking with fear I managed to do just that – I opened the door. Silence hit me – total and absolute silence; an empty room, freezing temperature, almost humming with silence. It was as if someone just flicked a switch and turned off a blaring radio. I ran for the door, forgetting the post and in a fumbling panic got out of there. I was shaking, almost hysterical when I got back to my office, so much time had passed that everyone was at their desks working. I never went into that room again; nothing would induce me to enter it. If ever I needed the loo, I would leave the office and use the facilities of Exchange Station.

Soon after I left that company and went to live in Portugal. Years later I found myself in Liverpool and discovered that the old chambers had gone – been pulled down making way for the new. And I wonder if the ghosts went with it, or have they somehow found their way into the new building?

Strange goings-on at the buildings to which Cathy refers have indeed been reported to me quite a few times over the years. A phantom bell and a pair of faint male voices arguing over something that just can't be made out have been heard in the newer buildings next to the chambers Cathy mentioned, but that is nothing compared to a man named Graham, who worked at 11 Dale Street – the very offices of the same Charles E Dolby Cathy mentioned in her chilling recollection. This incident took place in the early 1970s, when Graham was just seventeen and employed as an office boy at the firm; he ran errands, made the tea and posted bundles of letters. Graham had only been with the firm for three days when something quite bizarre took place.

It was a wintry morning and the teenager turned up for work at around half-past eight, and found himself lost. He went up several flights of stairs and found himself in a dark warren of old offices he had never seen before. In one of these offices, the flames of two candles could be seen flickering through the pane of frosted glass in a door, and Graham rapped on the door, deciding he'd ask whoever was in the office if he could direct him to his proper workplace. A voice commanded him to enter, and Graham turned the doorknob and went into the room to find a portly round faced man dressed in a black jacket, a white high-collar and odd-looking tie. He was hunched over the green leather writing surface of a huge oaken desk that was covered with stacks of books, scrolls tied with coloured ribbon, inkpots, and the two candles which Graham had seen through the frosted pane in the door. In his hand, the stranger held an antiquated feathered quill. He peered over the top of a pair of wire-framed spectacles and smiled at Graham. 'I've never seen you before, what's your name, boy?' he asked.

Graham believed the man was a ghost, that the dusty old-fashioned office was some phantasmagorical illusion from long ago, and so he did not answer the chubby elder's question, but instead, backed out of the room. He noticed the sound of horse's hooves clip-clopping outside, and the trundling of the cart or carriage which the unseen animals were pulling, and that really freaked him out.

Graham closed the door and hurried down the dark stairway, and eventually recognised the welcoming sound of an electric typewriter clattering away in the offices back in the twentieth century. When I asked Graham to describe the man seated at the desk, he said he was the spitting image of the actor who played the senior menswear salesman Mr Grainger in the old BBC comedy, *Are You Being Served*? I obtained a photograph of Arthur Brough, who played Mr Grainger until his death in 1978, and Graham said he was the double of the man he had seen. Graham and two workmates searched the building's corridors but never managed to find that old man or his office.

Another person, Steve Gibbon, who in the 1980s worked in an office in that same building, said he was astonished one day to see the name 'Pioneer Assurance Building' in gold letters on a frosted pane of glass in the vestibule door. He went to fetch his boss, but when he came back, the vestibule door was gone. In the 1890s, that office was indeed called the Pioneer Assurance Building. This whole area of Dale Street is steeped in ghosts and it comes as no surprise to me at all, for Hackins Hey, which runs alongside the haunted building where Cathy and Graham had supernatural experiences, is a very old and narrow lane where you will find Liverpool's oldest pub, Ye Hole in the Wall, as well as the Saddle Inn, which fronts on to Dale Street. Both of these pubs have their fair share of ghosts.

Staying on Dale Street, we come next to another series of fascinating timeslips which occurred in one of the city's most well-known and oldest pubs – Rigby's, which Horatio Nelson allegedly visited on several occasions in the 1790s. Rigby's, named after a former owner and spirit and wine wholesaler named Thomas Rigby (1815-1886), is said to date back to 1726, according to a date on its facade, but this date in all probability, refers to the earlier incarnation of the pub, when the premises were the Cross Keys. Nevertheless,

Rigby's is an old and very atmospheric pub and has been the scene of many strange goings-on of a paranormal nature over the years.

In the 1980s, Ann and Katy, two women in their early forties, called into Rigby's one day at noon during their lunch hour. Both women worked as secretaries at different local legal firms, and on this particular day, ghosts and the supernatural were the furthest things from their minds. All they wanted was a sandwich, a smoke, a bit of gossip and, of course, a little light liquid refreshment. The secretaries had only been seated for about ten minutes when Ann went to the toilet. The minutes dragged by, and Katy noticed her friend was taking a lot longer than she usually did, and so she went to the ladies' toilet and became very suspicious when she discovered that Ann was not in there. She asked two people she knew if they had seen her come out of the toilet, but though they had definitely seen her go into the toilet, neither of them could recall her coming out.

As Katy and these two people discussed where Ann could have gone to, the missing secretary came out of the toilet Katy had just visited. Ann looked pale and distant and when Katy asked her where she had been, Ann told her something very strange had taken place a few minutes ago. She had walked into the toilet and experienced some sort of dizzy spell. Everything had gone pale grey, and she had found herself in what she could only describe as some 'void of just nothingness'. There was no sensation of up or down, and no floor or ceiling or walls to be seen. It was as if she had just been floating in a grey fog, in a type of Limbo. And then, about a minute later, Ann heard the toilet door squeaking open, and the sounds of people chatting in the pub. The greyness faded and she found herself standing in the toilet, looking at the wall. The experience had been more baffling than frightening, although it was some time before Ann would venture into that toilet on her own again.

A few years afterwards, in the same pub, something took place which also defied explanation. Like the last incident, this one took place during the day, again around lunchtime. Harry, a man in his fifties who ran a newsagent in the city centre, went into Rigby's one rainy March day at around one in the afternoon. He had been serving in his shop since 6am and was now having a short break while his friend Tony replaced him behind the counter. Harry would then return to the shop around 4pm and serve till just after teatime. He usually had lunch at Rigby's or the Trial's pub.

On this day, Harry took an early copy of the *Liverpool Echo* into Rigby's and ordered a pint of bitter while he decided what he would eat. He wasn't feeling very hungry on this inclement day, and thought he might just have a packet of cheese and onion crisps instead of a substantial meal. He finished his pint, went to the toilet, and then, just before he came out of the gents, he washed his hands, and thought he heard a roar of loud laughter coming from the bar. He opened the door, and a strong smell of cigarettes reminiscent of the old Senior Service brand his father smoked wafted into his face. Now sunlight was streaming through the windows of the pub as if summer had suddenly arrived in the middle of March. Then Harry noticed something much stranger than the drastic change in the weather: the bar was full of military men; Royal Air Force men in blue-grey uniforms, army men and their officers, and all of the women were dressed in the style of the 1940s. The men, who were not wearing caps or hats, had their hair cropped short and slicked back with oil or Brylcreem, and the women had their hair styled as the women did back in the dark days of the Second World War.

Harry slowly made his way through the backdated drinkers and tried to find his seat and the *Liverpool Echo* he had been reading, and he soon saw that the layout, furnishings and seats were all different now. The barmaid who had served him just minutes ago was nowhere to be seen, and he recognised no one in the place. Harry began to doubt his own sanity at first, but then felt his stomach turn over when he realised he had somehow gone back in time over forty years. Outside the window were trams, and sandbags piled up against a wall further down the road, and an ARP warden crossing Dale Street. All of the people in the street were dressed in the style of the 1940s.

Harry took a deep breath and shook his head, and a tall broad-shouldered man in an RAF uniform gently patted his shoulder as he squeezed past him to go and talk to a group of men who were seated around a table. Harry thought he could hear a piano playing at this point, and decided to go outside.

In the street, the sun quickly faded in the sky, and with it the unseasonal warmth. Rain pattered against Harry's face, and he looked about to see a modern double-decker bus rolling past, followed by a white transit van. All of the people on Dale Street were now dressed in the style of the 1980s.

By now totally perplexed, Harry went back into Rigby's to find a man sitting in his seat, reading his copy of the *Echo*. There was no sign of the military men or the 1940s barmaid. Harry turned on his heels and went back to his shop immediately, where told his friend what had just happened. A customer overheard the conversation and said he too had experienced a similar timeslip in Rigby's in the 1970s, and had seen Teddy Boys come into the pub and attack a man who was dressed like something out of a black and white gangster film. When several customers went to the aid of the man who was being attacked, they saw him and the teds vanish into thin air.

One mild afternoon in February 2012, I was walking along Woolton Road with a friend, near to Our Lady's Bishop Eton school, when I happened to hear an unusual droning sound above and to the left. My friend and I looked up and agreed that the plane looked like an old WWII Messerschmitt. This plane disappeared into an unusual low cloud which had a faint yellowish tint compared to the other higher clouds. As soon as the antique plane flew into this cloud, the sound from its engine stopped immediately. I later received many emails from readers in Woolton, Wavertree, Old Swan, Childwall, Huyton, Mossley Hill, Aintree, Fazakerley, Anfield and Netherton, all reporting sightings of outdated planes flying over the skies of Liverpool. One man was driving along near the Fiveways Roundabout in Childwall when he spotted what looked like a Lancaster bomber, that lumbering giant of the skies, flying low over the rooftops.

A man in his eighties named George, heard the unmistakable whine of a well-tuned Merlin engine as he left the allotment on

Thingwall Road in February 2012, and looked up to see a Spitfire flying overhead. George's nephew also saw the outdated plane as it headed towards the south-east. George had seen and heard Spitfires when he was in the army, and knew without a doubt that one of those legendary planes had flown over Wavertree, even though the last operational Spitfire had flown in the 1950s. I immediately checked the newspapers and the net to see if there were any air displays involving World War Two aircraft in the region; there weren't any such displays being held anywhere in the North West.

A few years before this widespread aerial timeslip, I was contacted by a retired pilot who told me how, in the 1990s, he was flying a passenger jet high over Liverpool, bound for the Continent, when he almost collided with a Lancaster bomber. The pilot, co-pilot, and most of the aircrew saw the Wellington at such close quarters, they could actually make out the airmen sitting in the gun turrets. The jet's pilot took extreme evasive action, which shook the passengers up a little, and he, the co-pilot and crew agreed to say nothing about the chilling encounter and had to tell the ruffled passengers that the plane had encountered some 'air turbulence'. Had the captain of the airliner informed air traffic control of the encounter, he felt he would have been hauled before a psychiatrist and deemed mentally unfit to fly a plane. The encounter took place in the late afternoon with excellent visibility, and the Lancaster looked solid as it crossed the jet's flight-path, slanting down out of the clear blue sky, bound perhaps for the airbase at Burtonwood, in a bygone age.

We know, or think we know, that time is real, but what is it? If you happen to look at the clock and see the time is 9pm, then look again twenty minutes later and see it is 10pm, chances are, you will believe the clock and will not immediately suspect someone of turning the clock forward while your attention was elsewhere. Likewise, if you went into a coma and were unconscious for a month, you would believe a doctor if he told you that you'd only been asleep for a few hours. Time only seems to exist where there is consciousness, and I truly believe that the time is near when someone will make a breakthrough in our understanding of the time-space continuum and this discovery will probably result in physical time travel or a way of viewing the past through a television camera which can peer through a manmade rip in time or perhaps a 'wormhole', of the type now being discussed by physicists specialising in quantum mechanics, and when this technology comes to pass, the past will be opened up, and not just the distant past we know from history books, but the recent past, and that could mean that one day, the police will be able to check anyone's alibi by peering into the past to see if a murder suspect was really where he or she said she was at a given time. I imagine many politicians will not be too keen on such a prying device ...

THE MAN WHO WASN'T THERE

The following strange story took place in the winter of 1997 on Allerton Road, not too far from the legendary 'shelter in the middle of the roundabout' referred to in the world-famous Beatles song *Penny Lane*. Allerton Road has its fair share of charity shops, staffed by volunteers from all walks of life, and it was in one of these shops one bitterly cold and grey afternoon in January 1997, that Patricia, who was in her sixties, left her house on Dovedale Road and went to shop for a few items at Woolworths. By 3pm she decided she'd call into a certain charity shop for a quick browse. This shop had a little bookcase section full of hardbacks and paperbacks featuring all the well-told adult and children's tales from the writers most of us know – including a few we have never heard of. There was also a single cubicle with a swish curtain where Patricia liked to try on a second-hand dress or even a pair of donated slacks or pristine jeans given to the shop by some lady whose waistline or taste in fashion had undergone some change. There were children's toys in the shop too, everything from archaic board games from the pre-computer-console era to the Rubik's cube. Patricia still had a record player, and this shop always had a good stock of vinyl forty-fives, thirty-three-and-athirds – even the odd seventy-eight – which will be all gobbledygook to listeners of iPods and their digital music. Ornaments, shoes, racks of coats, cassette tapes of old ballad singers, nostalgic comic books, brass wall plaques, Guinness brand ashtrays, polka dot umbrellas, tiny piggy-banks with the words 'My Rolls Royce Fund' on their glazed hides, lost teddy bears, Crying Boy pictures, Newtons Cradles, Tuscany orange floor lamps, and the thing that had attracted the attention of Patricia: a Francie doll, with hair that 'grows', in the original orange and pink box.

A long time ago, around 1966, Patricia's daughter, Samantha, who was then five, loved that doll Francie. The two had become inseparable until Sam accidentally left the doll on a bus during an outing to town one day. She cried her eyes out and would never accept a replacement. Sam was thirty-six now with two daughters of her own. Patricia just had to get this Francie doll for her. It was just £2, and as Patricia waited at the counter to buy the doll, a man behind her said, 'You buying it back?'

Patricia turned and saw a man, aged about seventy-something, about five-feet three inches or less, standing there with a trilby, a brownish-yellow overcoat, baggy beige trousers, and a pair of shiny brown brogues. He had the brightest blue eyes Patricia had ever seen, and they were smiling eyes.

'Oh, no, this was never mine, ha ha!' Patricia said, and she grinned and looked at the boxed doll in her hand.

'People do that you see,' explained the old man in a soft voice, 'they bring things in here and then they get all sentimental and buy them back.'

'No, this is for my daughter. She had a doll just like this when she was a little girl,' Patricia began to explain, when the man interrupted her as he pointed to the shop window.

'You're probably too young to remember the trams,' he said.

'Oh no, I remember them well,' Patricia said, flattered at the man thinking she was too young to recall those antiquated green gleaming hulks.

'The terminus was over there, and there was a clock on the top of

129

that shelter. Do you remember the barber Bioletti over there?' the old man asked, and now his pale blue eyes really sparkled into life. Hailstones clattered on the window of the charity shop and the noise from the shower almost drowned out his words.

Patricia paid for the Francie doll and Sarah, the young woman behind the counter smiled and wrapped it in a plastic carrier bag, then, puzzled, looked to Patricia's left. Patricia turned to see what she was looking at. The old man in the trilby had turned to walk towards the cubicle – but there was a woman in there trying on a skirt, so Sarah shouted out: 'Er, sir! There's someone in there! Don't go in …' and before she could finish the sentence, Sarah let out a sort of yelp, because the old man collapsed into a heap of clothes. Patricia was witness to this incident. She and Sarah looked down at the floor, and saw just the toe of a shiny brown brogue peeping out from a crumpled brownish-yellow overcoat. Beneath the coat the women could see the pair of beige trousers, and lying neatly on top of this pile of empty clothes was the trilby the old man had worn. Of the old man who had existed just seconds ago between the hat and the brogues, there was no trace.

It was some time before Sarah dared to pick up the trilby, and she lifted it with an unsteady hand as if she expected the old man's head to be under it. 'You saw it, didn't you?' she kept saying to Patricia, who nodded unconsciously. Sarah left the shop that afternoon after phoning her sister in-law and asking her to come and fill in for her, just for an hour before the shop closed. It transpired, I believe, that the clothes the ghost had been wearing had been donated by his wife after he had suddenly dropped dead, from heart failure, on Smithdown Place, just a stone's throw from the charity shop. I have also heard that, every now and then, the nostalgic and solid-looking ghost performs this same vanishing trick at the charity shop, only since that day he only wears other people's cast offs, which makes the trick seem all the more baffling.

THE UNEXPLAINABLES

It's very satisfying to learn of a haunting, to look into the history of the house or place where the ghost was seen, and to resolve the matter by identifying the apparition through extensive research into censuses, old newspaper records, street directories, public records and so on, but there are so many reports that come my way which cannot be so easily resolved and explained, no matter how much research is undertaken, and the following stories are of this kind – the unexplainables I call them, and they are filed away under that name in my private records.

One rainy night in November 2010, a man in his fifties we shall call Bill, from Bagnall Street, Anfield, left his house and went round the corner of the street to the off-licence on Walton Breck Road, which, incidentally, is rather unimaginatively named 'The Offy'. Walton Breck Road was unusually quiet at 10pm, with just two cars passing down it heading in an easterly direction. As Bill was crossing the road he saw something large and dark to his right on the great square of wasteland between Venice Street and Varthen Street, where houses and shops once stood. At first, the Bagnall Street resident assumed the dark object walking in his direction was a large dog, but when he turned to face the thing, he saw it was not a dog at all, but a huge silhouetted bird, like a giant raven, waddling silently towards him on its four-toed feet.

Bill stopped in his tracks as he reached the other side of the road. This bird was, in his estimation, about four feet in height. May I point out at this juncture that Bill had not been drinking. In fact he had been painting his mother's living room walls all day and had been looking forward to a relaxing night with a bottle of wine, a big packet of Maltesers and a DVD. Bill swore under his breath, more out of fear than astonishment, and turned and walked back across Walton Breck Road and hurried on to his mother's house. He looked back at one point, expecting the sinister winged monster to be following him, but thankfully it wasn't, and Bill's mother Mary knew her son was not lying when he told her what he had seen because nothing got in the way of her son and his bottle of wine, and Bill refused to go back out the door that night, and he kept looking out of the window to see if he could see the oversized bird. He called a friend named David on Spellow Lane and told him what he had seen, and David, who loved mysteries of this sort, drove round to Bill's house, deliberately slowing down when he passed the piece of wasteland where Bill had allegedly seen the huge bird. David didn't see anything out of the ordinary there at all, and as much as he tried, he could not persuade Bill to join him and go out looking for the bird.

A few days later, Bill was in his local newsagents, Anfield News, when he overheard two women talking as they waited in a small queue. One of the women said her daughter had seen a huge bird walking up the middle of Baltic Street – the street next to Bagnall Street. Bill tapped the woman on the shoulder and said, 'Excuse me, love, I saw that bird as well,' and he told the woman and her friend about his encounter with the raven-like giant. 'Ooh, I wonder what it is?' said the old woman, and her friend shrugged and smiled, then said, 'There's no bird that big surely? Only an emu!'

Bill emailed me to see if I had heard about any such bird. I told him that a month before, I had received an email from twenty-two-year-old student, Kimberley, who had seen a massive black bird flying over Stanley Park. This was in early October at around 6.45pm. Kimberley and her friend tried to video the bird on their phones but it was too quick, and the student's boyfriend, a lad from Chester named Matt, tried to follow the bird on his mountain bike. According to Mike, quite a few people saw the enormous creature actually roost on top of Everton's Goodison Park stadium before it flew off into the gathering twilight – towards nearby Anfield Cemetery. It may be a black coincidence, but shortly after this, Bill, the man who first spotted the mysterious bird, lost his brother, who suffered a heart attack and died, at the age of just forty-three – and Kimberley's mother was diagnosed with cervical cancer, but thankfully, she made a full recovery after undergoing treatment. The enigmatic giant bird was compared to a raven by all who saw it, and the raven has always been regarded as a death omen. Of course, all black birds, as well as night birds such as rooks, owls, ravens and crows have always been regarded as omens of ill-luck, and on the subject of portents of death, I must include the following strange story among this baffling collection of inexplicable curiosities.

In August 1973, a number of people living in the streets surrounding Calderstones Park saw a white fox on the prowl after dark, and many of these witnesses subsequently died within days of seeing the albino-like animal. A woman walking her dog at 10pm thought a stray white dog was walking along the pavement on the other side of Harthill Road, until she noticed its bushy tail and the tell-tale profile formed by its pointed muzzle and distinctive ears. The woman's poodle tugged hard on its leash and barked furiously at the white fox, which stopped and looked across the road with its ruby red eyes. The woman later remarked to her husband that the fox seemed to wear an uncanny grin as it looked at her. It then ran off into the distance and crossed the road, heading for the gates to Calderstones Park, where it jumped a five-foot wall to gain entry to the park. Three days after this encounter, that same woman died in her sleep. Her husband was a superstitious man who believed the white fox had been some omen of death.

Other people began to see the snowy-coated animal; it was encountered by a milkman near Menlove Avenue, but he seems to have lived to tell the tale, and is still alive at the time of writing, but thirty-two-year-old Leigh – an amateur photographer from Woolton Hill – may have succumbed to the curse of the White Fox, and he had one of the strangest encounters of all with the creature. He was in Calderstones Park just before dawn one September morning that year, waiting to capture a shot of the sunrise over the trees, when he saw a troop of at least fifteen foxes, all sitting peacefully in a row, beneath the extensive spreading boughs of the oldest tree in the north west – the park's Allerton Oak, reputed to be around one thousand years old. The fox sitting right in the middle of the skulk of foxes was white. This was before the era of digital cameras, and so Leigh tried to fit his flashgun to his SLR camera but the foxes were alerted and ran off. Within a fortnight, Leigh died after coming down with a cold which then turned into full-blown pneumonia. Hours before he died, he suffered a number of nightmares about the White Fox and then slipped into unconsciousness.

The White Fox was seen again for a while in 1977, but not one person who saw it seems to have suffered any bad luck, and another white fox was seen in Calderstones Park several times in the 1990s. I heard rumours that those who had seen it had died in car crashes and all manner of gruesome circumstances, but, despite intensive research, could not validate any of these claims. Foxes only live for a few years, so it seems unlikely that the white fox encountered in 1973 was the same one seen in the 1990s – unless of course, the White Fox is some form of supernatural manifestation.

Calderstones Park is the place to view the enigmatic Calder Stones, Liverpool's most important archaeological relics – and where are they kept? In a locked greenhouse in the park! The six surviving stone slabs are thought to be about four thousand years old and the tallest stone is about eight feet high and three feet wide. The stones originally stood on nearby Calderstones Road, as part of an ancient burial mound. One of the first references to the stones is in the summer of 1568, when they were alluded to as the Calldway stones. Around 1765 the burial mound and the stones were disturbed and there were rumours amongst the locals that some malevolent force had been released when the ashes of the cremated people interred in the mound had been used as fertiliser by the tomb desecrators. The local ale went sour, a child was stillborn, and an ox fell dead for no apparent reason. Some believe the mysterious graven symbols on the Calder Stones are star maps, whilst others believe they were inscribed by ancient priests, not unlike the archetypal druid.

On 15 March 2012, a number of people in Allerton caught sight of a tall eerie hooded figure wearing what looked like a monk's cowl, standing (and some accounts say hovering) by the so-called 'Robin Hood's Stone', an upright slab of sandstone which stands at the junction of Booker Avenue and Archerfield Road, Mossley Hill. The stone is said to be one of the Calder Stones – and is around eight feet tall. The long scored lines which run longitudinally down the monolith have, over the years, been seen to give off an orange luminescence – possibly generated by piezoelectricity. In the time of Henry VIII some thought the long score marks on the standing stone had been made by archers dragging the heads of their arrows down the grooves to sharpen them, but the marks are, in fact, thousands of years old. In my opinion the stone should rightfully be placed back among the other stones, and those stones should ideally be put back in their original position.

Muriel Jones had been visiting a relative in Mossley Hill on the evening of 15 March 2012, and on returning to her home in Allerton, at around 10.35pm, she was walking down Booker Avenue when she noticed a tall figure with a pointed hood and a long robe which went down to the pavement, standing about three feet away from the Robin Hood's Stone. Sensing this outlandish figure had something sinister about it, Muriel Jones crossed the road and bumped into a woman she had known for years named Mary, who was out walking her dog. Mary said she had seen the figure earlier on that evening, at around 10.10pm, and as both women looked on, the abnormally tall 'monk' faded away into nothingness before their eyes.

Mrs Jones quickened her pace, believing she'd seen a ghost, but Mary went home and fetched her sceptical husband so he could see the weird figure for himself, and they found the monk back in the same spot. This was around 11.40pm. Mary's husband Ken walked across the road but kept a bit of distance between himself and the figure, sensing it was unearthly, and he quickly returned to Mary, saying he had seen the lower half of the thing's face, which looked grey. The couple made their way home as the monk stood stock still. Mary and Ken said they could not sleep that night because their dog kept barking downstairs, and they also heard their gate squeak five times, between two and four in the morning, as if someone – or something – was opening and closing it. Being mindful of the apparition they had seen less than three hundred yards away, they were too scared to look out the window to see what was playing about with their gate.

There are other unexplainables in my files, and we go back in time forty years from the last one to confront a creature I have written about many times before in my books. I'll tell you the story first.

When a man of the cloth tells you a story, you tend to give the narrative more credence than if it came from a regular member of the public, and the following story was related to me many years ago by a Catholic priest who is now retired, and we'll call him Father Connolly.

In March 1972 ten-year-old golden-haired Claire was supposed to attend a charity talent show put on by her school on the outskirts of Liverpool, but her brother was unable to give her a lift because he came down with mumps, and so thirty-five-year-old local priest Father Connolly turned up at Claire's house in the Paddington area of Liverpool at teatime, and patiently waited as the girl finished watching the last few minutes of her favourite television cartoon, *Touché Turtle*, and then he put the girl in his old Volkswagen Beetle before going back into the house to fetch Claire's beautiful dress for the show from her mum. When he returned to the car the priest found Claire was all giggly for some reason, and asked her why. Claire cupped her hand round her mouth and shook her head. The priest put her behaviour down to nerves, and drove off from North View and headed for Edge Lane. 'What song are you going to be singing for us, Claire?' Father Connolly enquired.

'"All Kinds of Everything", the song Dana sung, Father,' Claire replied, and the priest lifted his eyebrows and smiled as he nodded, 'Good choice. And you have a fine voice, and a beautiful dress, so you'll be on *Opportunity Knocks* next, I can foresee it.'

As the car passed the Botanic Park, Claire started giggling again and the priest said, all tongue in cheek: 'Laughing at nothing's the first sign of madness you know?' But then he also picked up a sniggering sound coming from behind him. 'Claire, is someone else in this car?'

Claire burst out laughing and nodded, and said: 'Sorry, father, my friend Brian wants to come to the show as well.' And as she said this the priest got the shock of his life, for instead of another ten-year-old, as he was expecting, a weird round green face popped up from the back seat. The face had large square prominent teeth set in a huge grinning mouth, a turned up sharp nose, small blue eyes, pointed ears and a burgundy-coloured beard. On his head, 'Brian' wore a black pointed cap. 'Ah, I'm sorry I gave you a start there, father,' he said. 'It's quite a mask isn't it?'

The shocked priest almost drove through a red light. Open-mouthed, he gazed at the weird goblin-faced child in the rear view mirror, 'Does your mother know you're going to the show, son? Why did you hide in my car?'

Brian let out a belly laugh, and Father Connolly could see that the supposed 'mask' Brian wore was far too realistic, and he went cold.

'That's no mask, you ... you devil!' the priest shouted, and Brian roared with laughter, and Claire joined in. The priest stopped the car, took his rosary from the glove compartment and turned to thrust it in the thing's face, but by then the entity had left the car. The priest heard the back left passenger door close gently, and he cautiously got out to see where the 'thing' had run off too, but could discern nothing of it in the darkness.

Claire burst into tears, and said Brian would never be able to find his way back home now and she asked the priest if they could go and look for him. The priest was too stunned to answer at first, then shouted, 'No, Claire, we are certainly not going to look for that abomination!'

Claire begged him to go and look for her 'friend' but Father Connolly ignored her pleas and drove off – turning the car through 180 degrees and heading back to Claire's house. The priest quizzed the girl about Brian all the way back but Claire remained as tight-lipped as her mother, who also said nothing when the priest told her what had happened. Father Connolly stood on their doorstep and blessed the residence – upon which Claire's mother slammed the door in his face. Mother and daughter still attended church after that but avoided any eye contact whenever Father Connolly was in the pulpit.

The priest never fathomed just what the thing was in his back seat that night. Claire's house, incidentally, was close to that part of

Kensington where leprechauns were reported back in 1964, and this latter incident has been featured many times in my books, including *Strange Liverpool*, in which I dedicated a whole section to the Little People sightings, called The Summer of the Leprechaun.

ENCOUNTER WITH A ZOMBIE

There are so many mysteries surrounding the Second World War, but one in particular always haunts my imagination. There were many veterans of the conflict who recalled some very strange incidents in the latter days of the war, as the once mighty Third Reich disintegrated. Russian, British, American and Canadian troops converging on Berlin encountered Hitler Youth and SS men who seemed impervious to machine gun fire. When some of these soldiers (many of whom were mere boys who had been brainwashed and enlisted into the Hitler Youth Movement) were seen at close quarters, some had bullet holes in their torsos and limbs, and horrific injuries to their faces, and yet they persisted in trying to defend Berlin from the might of the Red Army, as well as the British, Canadian and other armies of the alliance against the Nazis. After the war, some of the G.I.s and other soldiers of the alliance swore that they had fought zombies. One American spoke of seeing bullet wounds in a boy's face that had taken off his nose and blasted out his left cheek, revealing his molars and jawbone, and yet he did not seem to be in any pain, and appeared very calm and professional as he reloaded his rifle – until he was finally cut down by a carbine. More of these weird stories circulated after the war, of Nazi scientists injecting drugs into the boy soldiers of the Hitler Youth and soldiers of the SS to turn them into mindlessly obedient automatons, who could not be stopped by bullets unless they were actually decapitated or blown to smithereens by bombs – a zombie army, in effect.

It is known that Nazi scientists froze victims from the concentration camps until their body temperatures fell so low that they died, and then attempted to resuscitate them – always unsuccessfully. These were just some of the gruesome experiments carried out on the inmates of Auschwitz; other victims were submerged and once they had drowned, attempts were made to bring them back to life. It was claimed that if some method could be discovered to reanimate the drowned bodies, it could obviously be put to use where prized Nazi pilots had drowned after ditching their planes in the sea.

Since the days of Hitler, the conspiracy theories have raged over whether fluoridation of a nation's drinking water would make the average citizen slavishly devoted to those in power, and with or without mind control drugs in the water supply, we are all manipulated by the media and the internet to a certain degree, but true 'zombification' of the masses is still a few years away.

But what of real zombies, of the type we see in such tongue-in-cheek films as *Day of the Dead* and *Night of the Living Dead*? Well, I have written about a local zombie case in the *Haunted Liverpool* series before. In *Haunted Liverpool 7* I documented the strange case of the resurrected Victorian, Walter Slim, alleged to have taken place in 1971, and in *Haunted Liverpool 13* I related the creepy tale of a bona fide zombie created by a Haitian gentleman named Josué Beauchamp in the 1930s. The following true story unfolded many years ago in the 1990s, when two lads in their twenties, Ryan and Neil, went to the Cabin Club, which is located on the corner of Wood Street and Berry Street, just across the road from St Luke's, the 'bombed-out church'. Ryan and Neil went there specifically to meet members of the opposite sex, but instead soon became rather drunk, and at one point in their drinking spree, Neil tried to climb the big rocking horse that was a feature of the club, but fell on top of his friend. The two men, both from the Smithdown Road area of Liverpool, then got talking to a young black man who was of a similar age, and his name was Colly – but whether this was his first name or some nickname derived from his surname was never established.

Colly, Neil and Ryan ended up leaving the club and going to another one in the area where the music was mellower and they could hear themselves talk, and it was in this other club, on Seel

Street, where the subject somehow turned to the supernatural. Colly claimed that there was a weird underground flat under Paradise Street where an old Jamaican man practised all sorts of real magic. This subterranean residence was stashed with marijuana and all sorts of psychedelic drugs, but was said to be guarded by a real-life zombie. Ryan and Neil laughed when Colly told them all this, but Colly insisted he could validate his weird tale by showing Ryan and Neil how to get into the magician's place.

'Show us then, go on,' Neil challenged Colly, who then took them, at 2.30am, to an alleyway behind a crumbling warehouse near Duke Street. He climbed over a backyard wall and pointed to the window of a derelict house. 'You go in there and you go down to the cellar, and then there's a passage which leads straight to the magician's place,' he said, all matter of fact, as his eyes rolled drunkenly.

'Look, Colly lad, we're all too bevvied to go and find this underground place,' Ryan reasoned, 'so why don't we go down tomorrow when we're all sober, and I'll bring a torch as well?'

Colly reluctantly agreed, determined to prove he was not making it all up, and he went home to Toxteth after promising he'd meet Ryan and Neil on the following evening at 8pm. He didn't show up, but the pair went into the derelict house he had pointed out at 10pm, sceptical but curious. They did find a long tunnel which ran, according to their estimations, somewhere under Paradise Street, but as they explored it, Neil kept urging his friend to go back. 'This tunnel could cave in at any minute and no one would even know we were down here,' urged Neil, but his friend's curiosity had got the better of him and he carried on down the tunnel for about eighty feet, sweeping the feeble beam of a tiny pen-sized torch until he came upon an old wooden maroon door at the end of the passage. There was about five inches of water on the floor at this point. Ryan took careful steps through the muddied puddles, just in case they concealed a hole, and upon reaching the door, he turned its round brass knob. To his surprise, and to Neil's horror, the door opened. Straight away the two men were greeted by the scent of strong incense, and the dim orange light from a small solitary lightbulb that hung from the ceiling of a long corridor with bare sandstone walls. 'I'm off!' Neil whispered, and went to turn round, but Ryan grabbed his arm and under his breath, said, 'Shut up. Come on.'

Ryan led the way as they crept down the corridor which led to yet another passage which ran at right angles across the corridor. 'Left or right?' Ryan wondered out loud. He chose left, and found another door, about twenty feet further on, and this one was black, with a black handle on it. Ryan turned the handle, but the door wouldn't budge, so he went back up the passage and tried the other door, which was white with a black handle, and the door opened.

A sweet-smelling fragrance, mingled with warm air, assaulted Ryan's nose, and he peeped in to see a large vault with sandstone walls some twelve feet in height, and upon those walls were symbols and circles, scrawled in chalk and paint, and both men immediately felt these symbols had something to do with the occult. There was a dining table in the middle of the high-ceilinged room, covered with a fine white linen tablecloth, and in the centre of the table there were bowls of fruit and unused, unlit candles set in expensive-looking candelabra. There were two black-wooded chairs at the table and to the left of the table was a fireplace of some sort, bordered with black marble and a fire surround, and above the mantelpiece was an arched purple-tinted mirror in an ebonised and gilded frame, with floral cresting and a strange little horned head as the centrepiece at the top of the frame. 'Look, that fire's still lit, let's go!' Neil urged Ryan, but Ryan was entranced by the subterranean lair, but to reassure Neil he opened his jacket and pointed to the air pistol tucked into his trousers.

'What's that supposed to do?' Neil asked with a nervous smirk.

'It fires point-two-two bollies, that's what it does,' Ryan answered in all seriousness.

'Oh, well we'll be okay now, Ry, we're up against a black magician but we can fire ball-bearings at him,' Neil said, shaking his head. 'I'm off ... I've seen enough.'

Suddenly footsteps could be heard outside.

The two men froze and looked at the door. Ryan switched off the

141

pathetic weak-beamed torch and drew the air pistol from his belt. Neil was visibly shaking, and his eyes were fixed on the door with a look of utter terror.

'Get under there, quick!' Ryan pointed to the dining table, and Neil scrambled under the large table and watched the door from under the fall of the tablecloth as Neil joined him. The door inched open, and a pair of feet shod in Doc Marten boots stepped into the room. The door closed, and the feet moved towards the fire. The two explorers peeped out from under the tablecloth at the strange-looking man standing before the purple mirror. He was well over six feet in height, wore faded jeans, was stripped to the waist, and had large hairy-backed hands. His head was shaved, and his face was reflected in the mirror. The reflection was chilling. The eyes were the black eye-sockets of a skull, and the nose was non-existent – just a triangular hole. The cheeks were sunken, and Ryan and Neil could clearly see a stitched-up five-inch wound in the front of the neck as if someone had cut the stranger's throat just under the adam's apple.

Ryan and Neil were on the verge of making a dash for it when they saw the mirror change. The stranger's reflection faded away to be replaced by a weird scene. It looked like the viewpoint you'd see if you could look into someone's room via their mirror over the mantelpiece. Ryan and Neil could see the back of a clock and candlesticks on either side of the clock, which was resting on an unseen mantelpiece. The room reflected in the mirror bore no resemblance to the sandstone-walled vault; instead, the room it was decorated with cheap-looking woodchip wallpaper, and there was a rather scuffed floral-patterned sofa. A woman came into view, and walked right up to the mirror and looked into it, obviously oblivious to the man on the other side with the skeletal face. The woman was beautiful, in her mid-twenties. She leaned forward and began to squeeze a spot on her chin. There was a tiny spurt of pus that hit the mirror, and her beautiful face grimaced as she studied the yellowish-white spot before wiping it off her side of the mirror with her index finger.

Neil tapped Ryan on the arm and whispered, 'I'm going, seriously.'

Ryan nodded, and the two men crawled out from under the table on the side nearest the door. As Ryan pulled open the door, the grotesque-face of the thing standing before the mirror turned to the men, then ran towards them. 'Shit!' Neil exclaimed and pushing past Ryan, fled into the corridor. Ryan lifted the air pistol – and saw the silver ball-bearing roll out of the end of the barrel and fall on to the floor. He threw the air pistol at the face of the tall ghoulish man, and the pistol glanced off him and landed on the table. The fiend's face now had a crack running from the inside corner of the left eye, right down to the chin.

Ryan then sped down the corridor, and as he turned the corner, found Neil already opening the door at the end of the dimly-lit passage. The heavy footsteps of the skeleton-faced pursuer were getting louder, and Ryan ran as fast as he could. He ran up the flight of stone steps and out into the yard, and it was here that the two men came upon another very strange sight. A small black man, about five feet tall, was sitting on top of the yard wall. He had a maroon-coloured fez on his head, and wore some sort of dark green and black cloak. The man sat there, smiling, and when he saw Ryan leap up the wall to get away from the ghoul, he shouted: 'Babylon!' And at that moment, Ryan felt as if some powerful invisible hands were pushing against his buttocks, and he was thrown clean over the top of the wall and landed amongst the rubble and bricks in the entry with so much force, he was completely winded, and found it difficult to run, but somehow he managed to get away. As Ryan and Neil reached the safety of a well-lit Duke Street, they both heard the diminutive black man guffawing with laughter.

Days after this, Colly, the man who had first told Ryan and Neil about the underground room, was found dead in his bed from a suspected drug overdose.

Ryan and Neil never again dared go anywhere near that derelict house which gave access to the underground lair of the 'magician' and whenever they told anyone about their encounter with what seemed to be some sort of zombie, no one took them seriously.

However, many years later, when the massive Grosvenor Project got under way, entire streets were demolished to make way for the Liverpool One shopping complex, and during the excavations made to dig the footings for the new buildings, many finds of archaeological interest were made, including the uncovering of plague pits, parts of the old dock wall – and also the a strange vault under Paradise Street! The walls of the vault, believed to be some forgotten storage cellar, were covered with all sorts of unintelligible symbols. The vault was filled in, and all of the other things that were discovered in the excavations. The grave of Joseph Williamson, the so-called Mole of Edge Hill, was even found in that part of Liverpool years before, after being lost for decades.

Lord knows what else is buried under the streets of Liverpool – perhaps even the lair of a magician and his zombie sentinel.

THE FAMILY OF SOULS

On the last day of September 2009 at 6am, a girl with green, scarlet and black spiky hair buried someone who had been very close to her in the grounds of St James's Cemetery, a sunken churchyard dating from Victorian times which I have written about so much in my books. Over fifty thousand people lie buried there, a hundred feet below street level, most of them without a headstone, because the heathen city council moved their grave markers, monuments and memorial stones years ago. The girl with the tri-coloured hair was seventeen-year-old Madison, and the someone she was burying was Rosie, her beloved cat. Madison had found Rosie dying under the garden hedge after some low-life in a car had deliberately swerved to run her over as the frightened cat fled across the road. The grave digger was Charles, Madison's fourteen-year-old brother. She called him Charlie and he usually called her Maddie.

They both had a good cry after Maddie had stroked Rosie's head for the last time. The cat looked as if she was just asleep, and Maddie thought of those lovely summer days when the dust floated about on the shafts of sunlight as Rosie slept in her very own high-backed chair in the bedroom, often making funny little noises as she had a troubled dream. Maddie thought about the last time she had seen Rosie, going down the path under a starry sky, a few nights ago. The cat had looked back, and Maddie saw her best friend's beautiful eyes gazing back at her and never dreamt in a million years that she'd soon meet a slow and agonising death. Tears flowed through the teen's thick black eyeliner as she whispered, 'Bye, Rosie,' before covering her head with the thin end of the wide tartan scarf that had become the cat's shroud.

Maddie knelt there for a while, then looked up at Charlie, whose eyes were pink and watery, and he began to gently shovel the earth back into the hole. Maddie got up from her bended knee and walked away into a shower of falling leaves. She listened to the usual songs on her iPod as she walked away from her brother, numb with sadness. Her mother had talked about buying a new cat, but no one could ever take Rosie's place. Boyfriends came and went, crushes too, but no one had ever been as close to Maddie as Rosie, not even Charlie, and he was close.

'All that falls shall rise again. It's never over, Maddie,' said a male voice out the blue.

Maddie paused her iPod and extricated one of the earphones from her busby hairstyle. She turned to see that Charlie had been too far away to have said anything. He'd have had to have shouted from that distance, and anyhow it wasn't even his type of squeaky voice. This voice was soft and low, and much more mature. A falling brown oak leaf bounced of the tip of Maddie's pierced bottom lip and spiralled to the floor. There was an eerie stillness in the cemetery that Maddie felt such affection for – a tranquil silence that had crystallised around her. She coughed to prove to herself that she hadn't gone deaf.

In the distance, Charlie was patting down the earth with the spade, and also had the brains to put back the clods of grassy earth on the grave, so the ground didn't look too disturbed there. They both knew that there were sick people out there who would probably take great delight in exhuming the grave of a beloved pet, hence the earliness of the burial.

'Maddie ...' came that voice again, and this time her iPod wasn't even playing. Maddie turned around, and felt herself drawn to one particular blue-black gravestone amongst a row that lined the bottom of the grassy wooded slope which rises up to the great cathedral towering above it. She edged ever so slowly towards the gravestone, until she could read the name engraved upon it. The deceased's first name had been Thomas, and he had died in the late Victorian period, but the headstone didn't reveal how he had died, whether it was from a fever or if he had been murdered, or died in battle; it just said: 'who fell asleep on ...' followed by the date of his passing.

'Yes, that's where they laid me ...' said the invisible voice. Maddie was speechless, and slowly became aware of the sound of running feet. She turned to her right and saw Charlie hurrying through the morning mist with the shovel now wrapped in two black polythene bin-liner bags. 'You okay?' he asked.

Maddie said nothing, because she didn't want to frighten her younger brother by telling him about the disembodied voice. She walked alongside him out of the cemetery, the two of them kicking their way through the crisp yellow and brown drifts of fallen leaves, and the mystery of the voice somehow relieved the heartache of losing Rosie.

For the rest of that Wednesday morning, Maddie thought about Thomas as she lay on her bed, listening to songs by one of her favourite bands, My Chemical Romance. Maddie's mother came up and asked her if she wanted breakfast but she just shook her head and lay back on her bed. Her eyes settled on the poster of Hayley Williams, lead vocalist of the band Paramore, and after a while, she dozed off into one of those states of consciousness between sleeping and waking.

All of a sudden, she found herself in some dark room, with a candle flame flickering before her. Beyond that flame was a pale face. She knew instantly that it was Thomas, the young man who had been buried in St James's Cemetery well over a century ago. Maddie had a lot of dreams like this where she knew people and places she had never set eyes on before. This time she knew it was her boyfriend Thomas, and that they were in her other bedroom – the one in that other house before she had been Maddie, when she had lived in the 1960s. They had just come back from the Cavern club on Mathew Street, and had just made love, and now they were sitting round a table, dabbling in the occult. 'Look into the flame, Denise,' Thomas was saying. Yes, that was my name then, Maddie recalled with a sweet nostalgic feeling – Denise.

'Stare into that flame and look down the centuries,' Thomas continued softly, 'and see how we have always been together, soulmates from the Dawn of Time. We can never be apart; even death cannot keep us apart.'

'Thomas, I remember now, you and me forever and ever, and the Family of Souls!' Maddie cried excitedly; it was all coming back now.

'Yes, the Family of Souls, my love,' Thomas replied, moving in to kiss her. 'Charlie and Alex … and the elemental spirit Kar.'

Maddie recalled her cat. 'Oh, yes, of course, Kar! She was Rosie this time, and last time … who was she last time Thomas?'

'She was the dog we had … Kelly,' Thomas reminded her, 'so don't be sad because you lost Rosie – she always comes back to the Family of Souls …'

'Maddie!' said a young sharp voice.

Maddie woke sharply, and she could have throttled Charlie for waking her from the exhilarating dream. She swore at her younger brother and asked him what he wanted.

'Do you know where my *Call of Duty* Playstation game is?'

'I don't know! You had it last! Get out my room!' Maddie yelled.

'Emo!' Charlie shouted, and hurried from the room. He heard something that his sister had hurled at him hit the door behind him with a loud bang.

That afternoon, Maddie went to Grand Central on Renshaw Street, where she met her friend Claudia, who she had gone to school with before Maddie had dropped out because of a long bout of depression. Claudia and Maddie went to a café called the Egg on nearby Newington, and over coffee and chocolate cake they caught up on each other's lives, and eventually, Maddie told Claudia about the voice in the cemetery coming from the grave of a Victorian named Thomas, and of the strange dream about the 'Family of Souls'. Claudia didn't doubt her former school friend; instead she seemed very intrigued, and asked Maddie a strange question: 'Is it okay if I try and hypnotise you?'

'What?' said Maddie, rather taken aback by the odd request.

Claudia said she had been teaching herself hypnosis and had recently managed to put her mother into a light trance so she could remember where she put the house keys she had mislaid. Now Claudia wanted to probe Maddie's mind to see if she could get to the bottom of the mystery of Thomas and the supposed previous lives he had shared with Maddie.

'Ooh, I'm not sure,' said Maddie. 'I'm worried I might go into some trance and you won't be able to get me back out of it again.'

'Don't be daft, Maddie,' said Claudia. ' It's easy getting you out of the trance. Just give it a try, it's no big deal.'

So Maddie agreed to be hypnotised and the session took place in the attic 'den' of Claudia's home over in Birkenhead. 'That's one beautiful couch,' Maddie remarked as she ran her hand over the expensive long brown Vladimir Kagan sofa Claudia's father had bought for his daughter. Maddie was told to lie on the sofa and she did and Claudia pulled the roller blind down over the window and then began to induce the trance by asking Maddie to count down from ten to one, after telling her that each spoken number would make her more relaxed than the previous one. Then Claudia deepened the trance with her well-rehearsed lines from her book on hypnosis. Within minutes, Maddie was well and truly under the spell of hypnosis. Some people just can't be hypnotised, but a small percentage seem particularly susceptible to hypnotic suggestion, and Maddie obviously belonged to this latter group.

Claudia took her friend back through the years, and asked her what she could see, and Maddie obliged by describing her life seen through the eyes of a person of different ages. At last, Claudia guided her to the year 1992 – the year she was born – and Maddie startled her friend by describing, in vivid detail, her entry into the world; being squeezed from the warmth and safety of the womb, and then the blinding light of the room she was born into as she left her mother's body. Claudia urged Maddie to go even back further, and Maddie became silent for a while, then began to talk in a slightly different accent and at a faster rate than normal.

'What's your name now?' Claudia asked, and Maddie said it was Denise, and gave a surname too. 'What year is it?' Claudia asked, and straight away, Maddie replied: 'It's nineteen sixty-four.'

'Do you know what day it is, Denise?' Claudia probed, 'and the day if possible?'

'I think it's a Friday ... Friday the ninth of October,' 'Denise' replied.

Claudia asked her friend where she was and who she was with, and Maddie smiled, and her eyes flickered and exhibited what sleep-researchers term R.E.M. – rapid eye movement – caused by the eyeballs swivelling from side to side as the brain dreams. Maddie said: 'I'm with Tom, and Alex, and the dog Kelly. I'm in a good mood because we're going to the Cavern tonight. Tom likes John Lee Hooker and Alex likes the Bluesicians, and they're all at the Cavern tonight. We're in Tom's house in Everton.'

Claudia took her friend even further back, and now Maddie was in Nazi-occupied France during the Second World War, and Tom – now referred to as Thomas, had been arrested by the Nazi's because he was part of the French Resistance. Maddie was speaking in French, and Claudia could just about understand her, as her own knowledge of the language was very average. Claudia took Maddie even further back, and in Victorian times, it transpired that Thomas was dying of consumption, and during his funeral, a grief-stricken Maddie – who in that incarnation had been married to him – had tried to overdose on laudanum but a doctor had saved her.

Claudia took Maddie back through further reincarnations until her hypnotised friend spoke in a language she could not understand at which point, Claudia gently took Maddie forwards through time, and all the time, during this intriguing journey through some eleven lives, Claudia had been scribbling notes on a lined pad. When Maddie was taken out of the hypnotic state, she burst into tears, and said she wanted to kill herself so she could be with Thomas and her friend throughout the ages, Alex, as well as her beloved pet, Kar. Claudia had to drag Maddie away from the attic window as the girl tried to throw herself to her death. Things got so bad, the police had to be called, and an ambulance.

Maddie was sedated and was on the point of being sectioned by a psychiatrist, who severely reprimanded Claudia for dabbling with hypnotism. The psychiatrist claimed that Maddie had dreamt up the whole 'Thomas and the family of souls' scenario. Maddie had merely exhibited the extraordinary mental power of mythopoeia – an ability of the unconscious mind to fabricate stories which had no basis in reality. Maddie was put on all sorts of medication, and one evening, whilst still in the psychiatric hospital, the girl was astounded to hear footsteps approaching her bed after a nurse had just left the room. A tall man in a long black coat, carrying a top hat, approached her bed and knelt beside it. It was none other than her eternal lover – her constant soulmate Thomas, and his pale hands clasped Maddie's hands. He looked into her eyes, and his own green eyes seemed to glow with some sort of preternatural luminosity. He kissed Maddie's knuckle and begged her not to make any further suicide attempts. Where he and Alex and Kar existed there was no time, and so they were all prepared to wait for her – and Charlie too – until they all moved on to the next incarnation. Maddie sobbed and hugged Thomas, and he said he had only been allowed several minutes to 'come through' to be with her, hinting that he had begged some higher force to grant him this visit. The precious seconds soon passed, and when it was time to leave, Thomas promised Maddie he would always be looking down on her, always near, and then he said: 'I have always loved you, I love you now, and I always will love you, my eternal love,' and then he bid Maddie goodbye, and as he walked off, towards the closed door, he looked round one more time, and seemed to be in tears. He turned away and walked through the solid door to the private ward, and seconds later, that door flew open, and two nurses came into the room. They wanted to know who had just visited Maddie, because the two of them had just heard the footsteps of someone walking into the ward. Maddie just smiled now, convinced that she had not hallucinated Thomas and the family of souls, and she just said, 'Ah, you're hearing things ... you should be in this ward, not me.'

Maddie quickly recovered from her 'illness' and later returned to a life of relative normality. She still visits one of the graves of Thomas – the one down in St James's Cemetery – and she always leaves a single rose, to represent her undying love.

May I just tell you another story about the 'soulmate' phenomenon? Read on.

One late April afternoon in 1967, Greg Flint, aged forty, made himself comfortable with his copy of the *Liverpool Echo*; a cup of tea at his side, and a Woodbine cigarette to smoke, and the television turned down low in the background – pure bliss after working at an estate agent's office in Allerton all day. The time was 4.55pm, and one of Greg's favourite performers, Joe Brown, was due to come on any minute in a weekly programme called *Joe and Co*. Greg's dry lips had not even touched the rim of his teacup when something, which has never been explained to this day, took place.

The disembodied head of Betty, Greg's ex, appeared in mid-air, about five feet in front of him, and the strange apparition was surrounded by a bluish halo of light. Greg swore in shock at the ghostly vision. Betty looked as if she was in great pain – and then, as mysteriously as it appeared, the spectral form vanished into thin air. Greg was definitely not the sort to believe in ghosts, but he had a strong gut feeling that this was some sort of sign that Betty was either dead or in trouble, and reluctantly, Greg left his house in Fazakerley and drove nearly ten miles to her house on Hunts Cross Avenue. Greg knocked on the door, worried that Betty's husband Gareth – a huge Welsh brute of a man – might come to the door on the bounce, as he hated Greg having anything to do with Betty, but there was no answer. By this stage Greg was seriously wondering if he was losing his marbles. There was no question that he had been overworking recently – volunteering for extra Saturdays at the estate agents and helping out with his brother's business on Sundays.

Walking back down the path, he was stopped in his tracks when he heard Betty cry out. He turned and looked through the letterbox – and saw his former wife lying in a crumpled heap on the floor at the bottom of the stairs. 'Hang on, sweetheart!' Greg shouted. He hadn't used that term of endearment for years but it just came out naturally. He backed up, then kicked the front door hard. It flew open, and he immediately went to Betty's aid. She had foolishly put her hands in the pockets of her coat as she walked down the stairs, and stumbled. She had broken her arm and injured her back.

When Gareth came home late from work, a neighbour directed him to the hospital, where Greg stood toe to toe with him and warned him not to read anything into the situation. 'How did you know she'd fallen down the stairs?' Gareth asked, gritting his teeth, 'We're not even on the phone! Just passing by were you?'

A fight almost broke out until a nurse and a doctor intervened, and Gareth blamed Greg for making a scene, calling him a 'jealous ex' – and Greg was escorted from the hospital by the matron.

Almost a year to the day after this, Greg was in the bath, enjoying a relaxing soak – when he suddenly heard screams coming from downstairs. There was no mistaking it – it was Betty again, and she was screaming at the top of her voice. Greg jumped out of the bath, dried off as quickly as possible and within thirty-five minutes was pulling into Betty's house – just in time to save her, for she was being beaten up by a drunken Gareth. Greg booted open the front door, flew across the hall, and knocked out the wife-beater with one upper-cut.

It was not long after that, that Betty divorced Gareth and remarried Greg, a soulmate who was definitely on her 'wavelength'.

STRANGERS IN THE NIGHT

One night in August 2010, nineteen-year-old Kelly Louise Jordain of West Derby was invited to a party at her friend Sophie's house in St Helens. The party was going well until about 1.30am, when the copious amounts of alcohol that had been consumed began to make a few of the guests a bit argumentative. There was a remark made by a girl named Emma about Kelly's false eyelashes, and Kelly retorted by criticising Emma's 'plummy' coloured hair and this in turn led to Emma's boyfriend criticising Kelly's 'dated' ringtone. It all ended at 1.40 am with Kelly Louise throwing her drink in Emma's face. Sophie told her to get out, and then, after Kelly stormed out of the house, she noticed her phone's battery indicator was only two per cent full, and about to die. She tried to find taxi numbers in her contacts, but she couldn't and as she was halfway through asking the woman on the 118 118 service for a number to a taxi company in the St Helen's area, the phone died.

Kelly wondered how she'd ever get back to her home in West Derby, and by 2.00 am she was wandering along the East Lancs Road by the Rainford Bypass, trying to flag down a taxi. After about five minutes, a petite girl of around Kelly's age came walking towards her from Rainford Road, from the direction of St Helen's Cemetery. The girl was wearing a white dress that went to her knees, and she was barefoot. In her hands she held a pair of light shoes, Keds in fact. Her face was deathly pale, though her hair was reddish and fell to her shoulders. She smiled at Kelly and said, 'Are you trying to get home as well?'

Kelly thought there was something odd about the girl, but smiled back and nodded, before replying, 'Yeah ... why, what's happened to you?'

'I had a bad row with my fellah,' the girl said, and looked down at the pavement as she stood next to Kelly. 'I'm going home, I've had enough.'

'Where do you live?' Kelly asked, keeping her eyes on the few cars on the road at this time in case one of them was a private cab.

'Kensington,' the girl told her. At closer quarters now, Kelly could see she very young – probably younger than her, and she had freckles that were just showing through her make-up.

'Oh, Kenny,' said Kelly, 'that's miles away. If I find a cab you can get in with me and I'll get out at West Derby and you can just pay from there to Kenny if you want?'

'I'm skint,' the girl admitted, and seemed quite ashamed of it.

'How old are you?' Kelly asked.

'Seventeen, why? Do I look it?'

'Nah, you look about sixteen – you sure you're seventeen?' Kelly asked suspiciously.

'Yeah, turned seventeen in June,' the girl told her and looked up at last into Kelly's eyes.

'What's your name?'

'Brittany,' was the reply, and Brittany smiled and seemed almost embarrassed by her name, and asked Kelly what her's was.

'Kelly. Yay! Is that a cab?' Kelly shouted and waved and jumped up and down at the private hire cab passing by but it drove on into the night down the East Lancs, so Kelly gave it the single finger gesture. All of a sudden, a white lorry with the word 'Unigate' emblazoned on its side pulled up, and a bald-headed man peered out the side window of the cab and looked at Kelly and Brittany. He said nothing for half a minute, just stared at the teenagers as his engine ticked over.

'What are you looking at?' Kelly asked him, with an expression which lay somewhere between amusement and disgust.

'Do you two want a lift?' the driver asked.

Kelly just wanted to go home. Her feet were killing her, and she felt tired. She also wanted to see Brittany going home safely as well. She didn't trust the lorry driver, but as she looked at him, she started to get the feeling he was alright. He certainly didn't look menacing.

'I haven't got all night,' he said impatiently, checking his mirrors. 'You two want a lift or not?

'I'm trying to get to West Derby and she needs to get to

Kensington,' Kelly told him at last.

The driver nodded and told the girls: 'Okay, climb in ... and mind the traffic as you do.'

The teens climbed into the cab and then the lorry moved off down the East Lancs.

The driver looked straight ahead through the windshield and said: 'What are you two doing out at this hour in the morning? There are some maniacs about nowadays you know?'

'I've been to a crap party, and this girl's had an argument with her boyfriend,' Kelly Louise explained. Then she asked: 'Are you going to West Derby?'

'Near parts of it,' the driver replied, 'what part are you from?'

'Do you know Meadow Lane?' Kelly asked.

Without turning to look at her, the driver said: 'Meadow Lane ... is that off Muirhead Avenue?'

'Yes,' Kelly nodded vigorously, 'yeah, by the avenue.' And then she posed a question to the driver. 'Where are you going anyway?'

'Miles away, over to the Wirral,' he replied, and then he turned to Brittany and asked, 'You're a bit quiet aren't you?'

Brittany just smiled and said nothing. She looked out beyond the side passenger window at the nightscape scrolling by.

'She gave me the creeps when she walked towards me earlier on,' Kelly laughed with a sidelong smirk towards her young associate. 'She was walking from the cemetery. Thought she was a ghost.'

The driver slowed the vehicle and shot a strange look at Kelly, then asked: 'She was coming from the cemetery?'

Kelly nodded. It was as if he knew something odd about Brittany.

The driver turned to Brittany and kept taking alternate glances between her and the ribbon of tarmac that stretched into the distance. 'Where exactly have you come from tonight?' he asked the pallid-faced girl.

'Bleak Hill Road ... why?'

At this precise moment, for some unaccountable reason, Kelly felt goosebumps rise up on her fore arms and the hairs on the back of her neck prickle up. A very eerie atmosphere was filling the cab, and it

155

was now deadly quiet. Just the faint hum of the lorry's engine and the faint light from the green and orange luminous dials lit up the three faces in the cab.

'Bleak Hill Road; quite a distance from Kensington isn't it?' the driver asked Brittany.

Brittany remained silent, as if she didn't know what to say in reply.

'See this stretch of road here?' the driver said, nodding through the windshield at the section of the East Lancs near the Blindfoot Road junction. There was a ground mist rolling into the path of the lorry from the black unlit fields of vastness on either side of the motorway. 'Lots of times, at this hour in the morning, a couple – a man and a woman, both in their twenties by the looks of them, have been seen, arm in arm, skipping out into the road. I hit them one morning, round three.'

Kelly went cold. 'Hit them? You mean they died?'

'I hit them and I heard their bodies hit the bodywork,' said the driver, and he slapped his hand on the steering wheel to emphasise the impact with the couple. 'And I pulled over, and I saw his head jammed between the two front wheels. I nearly collapsed, as you can imagine. And then I looked again, and there was nothing there.'

'How?' Kelly was baffled by the driver's account.

'Spirits,' the driver told her. 'Spirits of a couple who had died on this road. They made a suicide pact for some reason, and got drunk, and then jumped out into the road in front of a juggernaut. Years ago. They're still doing it, but I don't know why. I think its like when something really bad happens to you and you are that traumatised, you dream about it, have recurring nightmares about it. The dead couple might be doing that. They might be reliving their deaths because of the shock. I don't know.'

Then the driver slowed the lorry, and cruised to a halt.

Brittany and Kelly looked at one another, perplexed.

'Why have you stopped?' Kelly asked the driver.

The driver was looking through the windscreen with wide eyes and a wide-open mouth, as if he had just seen something terrifying on the road ahead. Kelly and Brittany tried to follow the line of his gaze to see what he was looking at, but could detect nothing down the motorway that could instill such fear as there was on his face.

'You okay?' Kelly asked the driver, but he seemed rigid with fear, and the look of terror on his face was so disquieting, the two teenagers decided to get out of that lorry. Kelly suspected the driver was deranged, and when she and Brittany climbed down out of the cab, they clung to one another and hurried down the grass verge alongside the motorway. They looked back to see the headlights of the Unigate lorry slowly fade away – and then the vehicle faded away with the dwindling headlamps! Only then did the girls realise they had been riding in a ghostly lorry, and they shuddered. They walked and walked until they were lucky enough to spot a Hackney cab near the junction of Moorgate Road. Kelly told the cab driver what had happened, and after the taxi-driver had listened to her story, he said: 'Was this white lorry a milk lorry? Did it have Unigate written on the side of it?'

'Yeah!' said Brittany and Kelly simultaneously. 'How did you know?'

'That lorry has been seen by people on foot, and motorists, a few times over the years. I think the driver hit a man and a woman who were running across the motorway. The two of them were blind drunk. He killed them and then the lorry turned over and he died as well.'

I have heard about the phantom lorry of the East Lancs many times over the years, and of people being picked up by the vehicle's phantom driver. He always seems to stop, terror-stricken, when he reaches the spot where he died on that stretch of motorway.

Nanny's Secret

During a book-signing in 2006, an elderly, refined-looking woman named Marjorie told me a very interesting story about her grandmother, and I wanted to write about it immediately, but Marjorie asked me to withhold the story – until she had died. She believed she'd be dead within five years of meeting me, and sadly, she was to be proved right.

In 2011 her daughter got in touch to tell me of Marjorie's passing, and to remind me of the details of the intriguing account. Around the year 1900, Elizabeth, a lady of substance, from the Aigburth area of Liverpool, was widowed at the age of twenty-nine, and so a nanny was sought to look after her two children, seven-year-old George and five-year-old Gertie. Quite a few women applied for the job, but one of the applicants, Mrs Margaret Clarke, was quickly hired, for although she was from the working classes, Mrs Clarke seemed to have a very caring nature, but was also a very pragmatic woman. She was a strawberry blonde with threads of grey just becoming noticeable, and quite tanned, which, in the Victorian age, was deemed rather unappealing in the fairer sex. Mrs Clarke said she was normally as white as a lily but had become tanned through hop-picking in the fields of Ormskirk the previous summer.

The nanny's accent could veer on to the coarse side now and then, with some odd colloquialisms; for example, she called young George 'Jackaroo' and a 'larrikin', and always referred to the kettle as the 'billy can'. All the same, the children loved Nanny, and all of the servants got on quite well with her too. One day, after she had told George and Gertie a marvellous tale about the days when she sold lavender and shamrock outside the theatre in Williamson Square as a seven-year-old girl, George noticed the strange white mark on the side of her face, and asked her if it was a scar. She said it was indeed a scar from an occasion when a woman tried to disfigure her by throwing vitriol in her face.

'What's vitriol, Nanny?' George asked, and he was told it was a very strong acid that burned through skin.

'Who threw it at you?' Gertie wanted to know, and that point, Elizabeth, the children's mother and the mistress of the household, came into the nursery, and Nanny immediately stopped talking about the vitriol-throwing incident. Elizabeth felt there was something about Margaret Clarke she just couldn't put her finger on. It was plain to see that in her younger days, Nanny had been a beautiful woman, yet it was also obvious that she had been a real character in her day. Sometimes in the evening, the servants would stand at the bottom of the stairs and look up the flights of steps in awe as they heard Nanny's beautiful voice singing lullabies to the children. Elizabeth tried to get Nanny to open up about her past, but Margaret would always quickly change the subject. And then, one day, there was a visitor to the house who revealed her true identity. He was a retired magistrate, a well-travelled man named Edward, and upon seeing Nanny, his face became very pale, while Nanny's eyes widened with shock. 'Ah, so it is you!' Edward exclaimed upon seeing Mrs Clarke, 'You have come back!'

Nanny went to walk out of the room with her head bowed as tears streamed from her eyes. Edward turned to Elizabeth and said: 'Do you know who she is?' Elizabeth gave a puzzled look at the former magistrate when he referred to her nanny as Margaret, who now halted with her hand on the handle of the drawing room door. The retired judge gave a sadistic smirk, then projected his plummy stentorian voice – a voice that had condemned many a man to death – across the room at Margaret: 'In the annals of harlotry I doubt there is a name more famous than that of Maggie May!'

There was no gasp of disbelief from Elizabeth, but the face on the mistress of the house was priceless in the eyes of the quondam Justice of the Peace. There was a louring pause while Margaret froze at the door, as still and lifeless as a statue. She produced a handkerchief and after dabbing her eyes she turned to the smug snowy-haired man with a warning: 'You have cast the first stone, and I shall throw a rock back at you now, you old hypocrite!'

'Margaret!' Elizabeth recoiled, throwing her hands to her mouth.

Edward, the faded judge of people, clutched the arm rests of the ostentatious fauteuil as a cerise pinkness blossomed in his cheeks. His eyes bulged and he spat froth as he struggled to find a suitable reply to Mrs Clarke's outrageous threat, but before he could compose a sentence, the sharp-tongued nanny began to list, in great detail, the peculiar quirks of the old man's sexual behaviour.

'Enough!' cried Elizabeth, rushing to Edward to steady him as he lurched forward with his hand on his chest. 'You are dismissed, Mrs Clarke!'

'With pleasure!' Nanny roared, and she turned and stormed out of the drawing room and went to her humble lodgings in the eaves of the mansion to pack her things. As she left the house, she saw the family doctor arrive to treat the old judge's funny turn. George and Gertie were deeply upset when they learned that Margaret – or Maggie as they now called her – had been sacked, and Gertie burst into tears. Elizabeth told her little daughter that the nanny had said bad things to Edward, and Gertie asked what type of bad things and had they been true – and Elizabeth suddenly had a crisis of conscience. She realised that Margaret had understandably been hurt when Edward had revealed her shameful past and had merely fought back at the hypocritical person pointing the accusing finger. Oh, what to do?

Elizabeth immediately left the house to seek the advice of her friend, the Right Reverend Bishop Robert Brindle, at the newly-opened Church of St Charles. Bishop Brindle had been a friend of Elizabeth's late husband when both men served together in the Sudan campaign; Brindle as an army chaplain, and Elizabeth's husband as a captain. When the clergyman had heard of the thorny circumstances leading to Margaret's dismissal, he grabbed his coat and hat, and left his study with Elizabeth in tow, quoting an old Moorish proverb from his army days: 'Forgiveness from the heart is better than a box of gold.'

And so Elizabeth and the Bishop went in search of Maggie May. They visited Sefton Park, which was often frequented by many down on their luck who had no one to turn to, but Maggie was not there.

Just when the Bishop was about to give up, he happened to meet police sergeant Peter Miller, who had started to attend St Charles's Church, and Miller told him that a fair-haired woman had been seen walking into the river from St Michael's shoreline (the 'Cast Iron Shore') and now there was no trace of her.

On the banks of the shore, Elizabeth and Bishop Robert Brindle surveyed the river, dreading the sight of a body, but they saw nothing, and then came a familiar sound that lifted Elizabeth's spirits – the beautiful singing voice of Maggie May, drifting on the salty breeze across the shore of St Michael's-in-the-Hamlet – but from where? The Bishop pointed to an ancient fisherman's cottage. The sweet melody led them inside the humble single-storey abode of old Mr Shaw and his sister. Swathed in ragged (but dry) male attire beside the hob sat Maggie drinking rum and carousing. She had walked into the Mersey, intending to end it all – to be rid of her unfortunate past forever, but sixty-year-old Mr Shaw had swum out to save her, and he was very reluctant to let her go when Elizabeth begged Maggie to come back to the mansion, but come back she did, and she was doted on and given the best fireside chair and a bowl of some mustard concoction to place her feet in as she warmed her bones.

Elizabeth apologised for dismissing her, and Maggie asked if Edward the old magistrate had recovered. Elizabeth said he had, and as the flames danced in the coals of the grate, the Bishop listened to Nanny's potted history of her life:

'For as long as I can remember, I always sang. Used to sing myself asleep when I was a child. I lived with my mother and stepfather off London Road, and when mam died he started to beat me. He used to throw me out on to the streets to make money for him. This was when I must have been six. I sold shamrock and lavender outside the New Star Music Hall (now the Playhouse Theatre) in Williamson Square. I got the best business outside the Walker (Art Gallery) and the Royal Alexandra (now called the Empire), but I got my break outside the New Star on Williamson Square. Dan Saunders owned it, and he heard me singing outside the stage door. He came out and asked me what my name was, and when I told him he said, "Little

Maggie May, you're going to be on the top of the bill one day," and he took me inside the theatre and gave me lemonade and Eccles cakes, and he sat at a piano and told me to sing a song. I was shy and my face was flushed and my throat dried up. But Dan was lovely, and he told all the actors to go away, and they did, and I started to sing.'

'What did you sing, Maggie,' asked the Bishop smiling softly.

Maggie's reddened eyes, full of sorrowful reverie, seemed lost in the glowing coals. 'I sang this, Bishop,' she replied, and began a soul-stirring rendition of *Amazing Grace*. Then Maggie continued her narrative. 'I got home late from the music hall, and my stepfather beat me. He was drunk, and threw me out. That night I slept on the steps of St George's Hall, sheltering from the rain. I used to sleep there a lot when he threw me out, and always had this same dream – that mam was alive, and she'd always be cooking in the kitchen, as she used to do, making stew and sometimes pudding. I loved those days when I helped her in the kitchen. Mr Saunders kept giving me lessons and then he put me on the stage as "Little Maggie May" and something amazing happened ...'

Little Maggie May, as the child was billed, was a natural on the stage of the New Star Music Hall, and the audience adored her. At first the little cherub from the grim streets of Liverpool stood stock-still, centre-stage in the limelight, until some critic in the audience began to shout, 'Move about will ye, child?' And Maggie began to skip around the stage to hilarious applause. In the wings, professionals such as the high-earning clown William Wallett (known as Queen Victoria's Jester) and the Chantrell Family of Acrobats, recognised new talent when they saw it, and Wallett knew Little Maggie would be a hard act to follow – and he was right. After her ten-minute spot the child received a standing ovation, and the stage was showered with coins. When Wallett came on he was booed and someone pelted him with a dead duck that had been smuggled in from the market. Every performer lived in mortal fear of being struck with this feathered symbol of the audience's displeasure. Little Maggie May was instructed to sing *Amazing Grace* and was literally pushed back onstage by Dan Saunders, the owner of the music hall.

Hats were launched into the air and the crowds cheered. 'Give us *Sweet Molly Malone!*' someone shouted, and Little Maggie May happened to know the old song word for word, for it was a favourite of her late mother's, and so she cried towards the end, thinking of her mammy, and there was not a dry eye in the house when the crowd saw the child shedding real tears. 'Encore!' the audience chanted, and Maggie gave a courtesy bow. The audience surged forward, some clambering over the musicians in the orchestra pit to shake the girl's doll-like hand, and pandemonium broke out. Dan Saunders had to come out on stage and with his hand on his heart, solemnly promise the crowds that Little Maggie May would become a regular feature at the New Star Music Hall. 'One more, one more!' the crowd chanted and stomped in time. Saunders bent down and asked, 'Maggie do you know any more songs? We're in trouble if you don't, girl.' Maggie said she knew *Greensleeves*, and so the orchestra was briefed, and the crowds returned to their seats.

In the forests of the printed word, much has been written about the great vocalists from the enchanting Sirens of Ancient Greece to the twentieth century's Maria Callas, but when Little Maggie began to sing *Greensleeves* a cappella – with the full orchestra poised to accompany her after the first verse, time stood still in that Liverpool theatre, and people later swore the performance was almost a religious experience, as if an angel had been allowed an earthly audience.

Little Maggie's May's future was made, or so it was widely thought, but in the wings, standing in the shadows, stood a man known as Flowery Jack, the notorious 'King Pimp of Lime Street'. He saw a great future for Little Maggie as well, and he bided his time, and when the child's star began to set during her teens – when the management of the music hall changed hands, Flowery Jack moved in and took a blossoming Maggie May to Lime Street's Crown Hotel to launch her career – and a legend was born.

At this time, the Queen of the Harlots was Polly Hogan, but then teenager Maggie May, crowned with red roses and a fine scarlet dress, came into the pub – and sparks soon began to fly.

Sixteen-year-old Maggie May was introduced to the staff and

motley drinkers of Lime Street's Crown Hotel by the refined pimp Flowery Jack, and many couldn't believe that the tall beauty before them was the same girl who had made them laugh and cry in the New Star Music Hall just a few years ago. Was this really the little girl who now stood before them? What a vision she presented with her golden hair elaborately styled, her flawless pale porcelain skin and those huge expressive eyes and that striking shapely figure. Maggie wore a crown of roses in her hair, and a beautiful blood-red velveteen dress adorned with rose motifs. On her feet were scarlet satin ballet shoes. She held half-unwrapped gifts from a multitude of admirers in her arms and the male drinkers swarmed around her. One man named Jackson, who had returned from the United States, presented Maggie with a real gold nugget, which she dutifully handed to her 'promoter' Flowery Jack.

Up until this day, thirty-seven-year-old Polly Hogan had been the unofficial Queen of the Harlots, and she gritted her ivory dentures as she eyed up her obvious replacement. To her little four foot eight inch friend Geraldine Faylin, Polly declared: 'Well, Ged, I'll jolly well be hanged if she thinks she's taking over my pub,' said Polly in her nasally cocksure style, the product of her long nose and untreated adenoid condition. Little Ged Faylin thinned her almond shaped eyes, which were set in a pink round face and looked up at her friend: 'Shall I splash her with something, my dear Polly? Melt that pretty face of hers?'

Polly's huge brown eyes darted left and right, and she slapped her hand over Ged's mouth. 'No, love, you don't have to do that – not yet.'

Jealous Ged, as the dwarf Geraldine was known, loved nothing more than buying a penny bottle of vitriol (sulphuric acid) from the chemist to hurl into some beauty's face in a suitably dark alleyway. Polly jostled her way through the crowds of mesmerised men of all ages who were swarming round Maggie, until she came face to face with her perceived Nemesis. 'So you're the famous Maggie May, are you?' she asked, speaking from the back of her nose.

Maggie said nothing, but her faint Mona Lisa smirk and the way her heavy-lidded eyes looked Polly up and down, plainly told everyone that she was not even considered a threat to such youth and beauty; no competition! Maggie turned her back and Polly shouted: 'How the bleedin' mighty have fallen! Little Maggie May turned streetwalker!' And the Crown's new owner, Billy Barton, came running from round the bar to tell Polly to 'shut that vile trap' – as Maggie May suddenly turned round and launched a punch that knocked out Polly's ivory dentures. The crowd cheered as Polly fell heavily – onto little Ged Faylin, who screamed nasty threats of disfigurement at Maggie, and Flowery Jack told four burly men to lift Maggie on to their shoulders – which they did. 'Hip-hip hooray!' Jack yelled thrice, before gleefully announcing, 'Drinks on the house! God save Maggie May, the new Queen of Lime Street! Now let's tell them at the Vines, lads!'

And Flowery Jack and a formidable mob (many of them members of the High Rip Gang) carried Maggie out of the pub and down Lime Street to the Vines pub to confirm her 'coronation'.

Back at the Crown, Ged Faylin told her unconscious friend through gritted teeth, 'I'm bled if she thinks you're finished, Polly,' before sneaking out of the pub, intending to get the bottle of acid.

Maggie May's coronation was cautiously accepted by the management of the Vines – a drinking establishment named after its manager, Joseph Vines, a very shrewd businessman who turned a blind eye to Lime Street's sisterhood of harlots. This was what some of the men came for; the sailors, the labouring men, as well as the slummers (toffs disguised as working people) – they came not only for the drink and the conversation and the singalongs, but also for a temptation that stretched back to Genesis – the pleasures of the flesh.

Flowery Jack, Liverpool's most famous pimp, was suspiciously absent as everyone gave a toast to Maggie May, and a few minutes into the celebrations he came into the Vines with his 'wide-awake' hat stylishly slanted, adjusting the perfect rose backed with maidenhair fern in his lapel. He went straight up to Maggie and took her behind the bar into the manager's room, where he explained the 'situation': 'There's a very well-to-do man outside in a carriage. He's a good client of mine and he wants you and another girl, so are you all right with that, me dear?'

Maggie May looked afraid. This was her first customer. All the bravado had evaporated. 'What do you mean ... me and another girl?' she asked Flowery, and he put his index fingertip on her lip and said, 'There's nowt queer about that, now let's be going ... and none of your swearing; this gent's an educated toff.'

Flowery took Maggie to Bolton Street at the back of the Vines and there the silver-tongued procurer was paid in an alleyway by the tall top-hatted gent, who said, 'Come,' and curled his index finger, beckoning Maggie to accompany him into the black lacquered carriage. Maggie looked nervously back at Flowery, who waved her off: 'Go on, he's a gent! You'll be alright, my love.'

Imagine Maggie's face when she stepped up into that luxurious carriage, only to see the top-hatted upper-class gent sitting next to none other than Geraldine 'Ged' Faylin – the mad midget who had wanted to throw acid in Maggie's face.

'What's *she* doing here?' Maggie asked, but the gentleman just smiled and reached up to the little hatch in the roof. He slid back a small door and gave instructions to the driver, and the carriage moved off. 'She has a fascinating face,' said the well-heeled client in a perfect Queen's English accent, and his long pale fingers stroked Ged Faylin's little cup face. The little thing smiled as he did this. 'What an unusual birth-mark!' he said, inspecting the black mole at the corner of Ged's lip. Maggie asked the man what his name was, and he told her it was Jerome.

'And what is it that you do, Jerome?' she asked.

'I'm a surgeon,' he replied.

Nothing more was said throughout the long journey to a mansion off Edge Lane, even though Maggie threw many questions at Jerome. She just wanted to jump out of the carriage and go back to singing on the stage. At the mansion, Ged Faylin was taken to another room in the grand abode, and Maggie was taken to a room with the word 'Wednesday' printed in gold on its door. 'You shall be Wednesday,' Jerome told her, lifting Maggie's chin, 'that shall be your name from now on.'

Maggie noted the other doors along the deep-carpeted corridor – all named after other days of the week. 'My name's Maggie, not bleedin' Wednesday!' she protested, unaware of the horrors she was about to witness.

Hours passed in that well-furnished prison of a room in Jerome's Edge Lane mansion, and at last Maggie was summoned to the surgeon's vast master bedroom, where the illustrious client waited naked in his four-poster. Maggie arrived in the dark chamber to find Jerome sitting up in bed, puffing on an opium pipe. The sharp smell of the opiate was well known to Maggie and always made her sick.

'Divest!' Jerome barked, and at this point Maggie noticed a large jar on a cabinet beside the bed. By the dim scarlet lamp, she could make out something organic inside that jar. Oh my god! It was the pickled body of the midget Faylin. The little shaven-headed corpse gawped lifeless at Maggie from the jar with her large sad eyes. As Maggie started to back out of the room, Jerome told her that Faylin had choked to death at supper, and he had merely put her in a solution of formaldehyde pending an autopsy, as if such behaviour were totally commonplace. But Maggie didn't believe him for a minute, and suspected that he had killed her to satisfy some sexual aberration of his – to have sex with a corpse at his bedside.

Seized with panic, Maggie ran off, and somehow escaped from that house of death to make her way back (through torrential rain) to Flowery Jack's house on Cumberland Street. Flowery would not countenance the idea that the surgeon was a murderer and angrily declared that he now had no choice but to place Maggie in the care of another pimp in London, or Jerome would come after her for defaming him.

Maggie was subsequently placed in an upper-class Mayfair brothel, where she mixed with the top courtesans of the day such as Liverpool-born Catherine Walters (known as 'Skittles'), Cora Pearl, and Marguerite Bellanger (mistress to the Emperor Napoleon III). Maggie became privy to the greatest secrets and hidden scandals of high society – even of royalty – and one day she told a regular trusted client about the clandestine night-time weddings of the 'Uranians' (a secret sect of distinguished men of standing who, by law, had to keep their homosexuality hidden in Victorian times).

When this 'scandal' broke, Maggie May was forcibly exiled to Australia (but not Van Diemen's Land as the old song says). Here, Maggie's name was changed to Clarke, and she lived in obscurity in Sydney and Adelaide until all of the people involved in the scandals had died, and only then was it deemed safe for her to return home. People Maggie had known back in Liverpool wondered what had become of her, and soon the famous ballad writers of the town penned a bawdy folk song to try and explain the famous harlot's absence. Maggie would cry bitter tears when that cruel song reached the shores of Australia, for she had never robbed anyone.

Maggie May had returned to Liverpool as a nanny by 1900, and although a retired judge insensitively unmasked her as one of the most famous prostitutes in the world, Maggie's employer, Elizabeth, her friend Bishop Robert Brindle, and Elizabeth's two children, George and Gertie, all loved her. Maggie often returned to the Crown Hotel, the Vines, and Liverpool Playhouse, no doubt to reminisce on her astonishing life.

Sometime in the 1930s, Maggie passed away and for many years, people spoke about the incredible funeral cortege – a long train of cars behind the grand looking black carriage that took the legendary lady to her grave – said to be up in Ford Cemetery. Some of the older people who had known Maggie stood solemnly at the roadside, doffing their hats and waving at the hearse.

I often wonder if the little ghostly female urchin often seen sleeping against one of the pillars of St George's Hall is the phantom of Maggie May as a child, for she slept there when her stepfather threw her on to the streets at night. I will set out Maggie's full life story in a book one day, to set the record straight and to pay homage to Liverpool's forgotten courtesan.

PET HOLE

As incredible as the following story may seem, it is, as far as I have been able to establish, backed up by the testimony of quite a few people. I have had to change a few names for legal reasons.

Once upon a time, many years ago in the 1970s, there lived a rather lonely nine-year-old child called Colin, who lived with his mother, grandmother and uncle in a fifteen-storey tower block near William Henry Street. This tower block was one of three that were known by the infamous nickname of 'The Piggeries' because vandals had destroyed all its amenities. The hooligans removed light bulbs from the staircases, turning them into treacherous pitch-black death traps, especially for women, who had to somehow drag prams up the fifteen storeys, because the lifts rarely worked, and even when they did, the vandals would defecate and urinate in them. Each of the dystopian blocks housed seventy families, and the flat Colin lived in was on the top floor, fifteen storeys up.

Colin was not really aware of the high-rise slum he was living in; children are often insulated from a harsh reality by their childish perception; it's as if they inhabit a separate universe to the seriously-minded adult.

Anyway, one day in the early 1970s, just a week before Christmas, Colin was playing with his toy balsa wood plane, holding it up in the air and steering it across the living room as his grandmother watched the television. The time was around two in the afternoon. Colin put down the balsa glider with its rubber-band operated propeller, and gazed out over Everton wondering where his father had gone. He had just upped and left earlier in the year, and Colin missed him terribly. Colin's dad used to tell him stories before he went to bed each night, and nowadays when Colin asked his mother to do the same, she'd always say, 'Oh, I don't know any stories, Colin, now get to sleep.'

Colin lifted the net curtains and was gazing up at the grey overcast skies over the city – when he noticed something. A tiny green light – just like the twinkling fairy light on the Christmas tree – was floating down from the sky. 'Nan! Look at this!' he shouted, excitedly pointing to the descending light. But she was too engrossed in the Abbott and Costello film she was watching to be bothered getting up from her armchair. The light floated down towards the window next door – the window of Colin's bedroom – so he raced out of the living room, through the hall and into his bedroom to witness the dramatic entry of the 'thing' into his life. The bright twinkling light hit the window and went straight through it, its light extinguishing as it hit the windowsill – and it left a faint grey dot there in the white paint of the sill. Colin hurried across the bedroom to get a better look. It was a pale grey disc, the size of a half-penny piece, and it was moving across the windowsill.

Colin put his hand next to the edge of the windowsill and brushed the grey disc on to his palm.

He got the shock of his life. There was now a hole in his hand the size of a half-penny coin. He held his hand up to his face and looked straight through the hole in his palm, which had a red blood-coloured edge to it. Then this grisly peephole moved across Colin's palm towards his thumb. Colin couldn't make any sense of what he was looking at, but his childish mind accepted that he was holding a hole that could actually move about and had some sort of intelligence controlling it. He ran in to show his Nan, and she squinted through her glasses at the moving hole and said, 'What is it? I can't see what you're showing me, Colin.'

'I've got a pet hole, Nan,' Colin told her and giggled.

His Nan, like her daughter, Colin's mother, was a woman of no imagination or curiosity. So instead of showing amazement, or wonder, she turned her head back towards the television as if Colin hadn't said a word and began to chuckle at the antics of Abbot and Costello.

At teatime, Colin's mother came in from work and found her son eating all sorts of sweets and bars of chocolate in his room, and she immediately asked him where he had obtained the money to buy these goodies. Colin seemed stuck for words, caught off guard with a mouth ringed with chocolate. Then after managing to swallow the mouthful of Maltesers he had just stuffed in his mouth, the told her that he had found a five-pound note on the landing outside the flat.

'I don't believe you,' said his mother. She knew just from his expression and flushed face that he was lying. 'Now where did you get the money for all this? Hey? Have you been stealing it out of your Nan's purse?'

Colin tried to tell her the truth: he had put the hole on the glass cabinet in the sweet shop, and the hole had expanded and let him help himself to whatever he wanted from the cabinet. Colin's mother was furious, 'Tell the truth or you're going to bed!'

Colin repeated his seemingly far-fetched story as he couldn't think of anything else to say since it was the truth, and so his mother stormed off to his Nan and asked her to check her purse, as she thought Colin must have taken some money from it. Nan checked the purse and saw that nothing was amiss. This worried Colin's mother, for now she thought he had stolen the money from someone else. Because she couldn't get to the bottom of the mystery, she grounded Colin and he had to stay in his room for the rest of the day and, of course, she confiscated what was left of the sweets.

The boy couldn't put the grey disc-shaped 'pet' down. He stroked it and sometimes it felt like glass and like jelly at other times. Sometimes it felt as if it was vibrating, a bit like a cat purring with satisfaction as he stroked it. Getting more adventurous, Colin laid the hole on his arm and began to poke through it with a pencil tip, but all of a sudden he felt excruciating pain in his arm, and a spurt of blood came out of the hole and splashed his face. He winced with the pain, but then the hole closed up leaving no sign of injury to the skin, just bloodstains on his arm and splashes of blood on his face.

Now rather more wary, Colin tried to put the hole away in a matchbox for a while, but it couldn't be contained by anything, because of its strange topological nature. In the end, the hole crawled back through the windowpane, and out on to the window ledge, where it became a bright green point of light and floated away, up into the sky, until it was lost among the greyness of the low oppressive December snow clouds. Colin cried out for his 'pet' to come back, but he never set eyes on the strange entity after that day.

The owner of the local sweetshop later told Colin's mother about a strange hole that had appeared in the cabinet where his chocolate bars and other sweets were on display. The hole seemed to expand and shrink as he looked on and he didn't know what to make of it. Colin's mother had also seen the tip of her son's middle finger vanish when he had tried to show her the unearthly object. Colin's friends also saw the eerie hole in action as he let it crawl over their hands. We'll probably never know what the hole was; perhaps it was some visiting alien life form, or some entity from a higher dimension as it certainly seemed to possess intelligence. As Shakespeare said, 'there are more things in heaven and earth ...'

EVE AND LIV

Everton versus Liverpool at Wembley is, without a doubt, a landmark fixture and a sporting event (dare I say it?) to even eclipse that other local but global event of the sporting calendar – the Grand National. The rivalry between the supporters of the two clubs, whose grounds are within a mile of each other in this football-crazed city, is fierce. The polarising pull of Everton and Liverpool can divide families and even the closest, most intimate couples in a way that defies any anthropological analysis. I have even seen priests in heated arguments after a Derby game. Most people in Liverpool are born Red or Blue, and should a geneticist scrutinise the human genomes of the people of this city closely enough he would find 'Nil Satis Nisi Optimum' or 'You'll Never Walk Alone' encoded in their DNA. To say football is a passion in Liverpool is a clichéd understatement – it's a religion – possibly a throwback to the ancient Celtic Druids.

Long before St Augustine brought Christianity to these shores, the Roman vanguard saw mad-looking ancient tattooed Britons, one group with their skins dyed blue with woad and the other tribe stained red with an iron-based pigment called vitrum, and they were kicking animal-hide prototype footballs about under the supervision of a druidic overseer (a referee).

Football, then, is part of the shared race memory, embedded in the collective unconscious, a metaphysical ritual, a devotion, and that often misquoted line about Shankly saying football is much more important than a simple matter of life and death is truer than we think: he was citing a scripture. The love of the game even transcends death itself.

Many years ago, in 1984, the year the Reds and the Toffees met twice at that cathedral of sport, Wembley, there lived two friends, Matty and Stan, red and blue respectively, both aged twenty-two. The young men were the closest of friends, but their families took their love of their opposing teams to extremes. Their houses faced one another, and a fortnight before the FA Charity Shield game at Wembley, things escalated. Matty was forbidden to associate with Stan, and vice versa. However, the lads bumped into one another in town one Saturday night in the Philharmonic pub, where they met two of the most beautiful girls they had ever seen. Eve was a supermodel in the eyes of Matty, and Liv was like some sultry Hollywood starlet to Stan, and the newly formed foursome set off on a tour of all the city's clubs, and love really was in the air.

'We'll take them to Wembley,' Stan told Matty, after escorting the girls home.

'Played! Good idea, Stan lad.'

The families of Stan and Matty yawned when the lads told them they had each found 'the one', they'd heard it all before. But soon there was talk of weddings at Anfield and Goodison, and then one day, in Hardman Street's Kirklands wine bar, over a pint of lager and 'expensive scran' as Matty called it, Eve revealed her name was short for Everton, and Liv then laughed with a startled expression at this disclosure, because her name was short for Liverpool, not Olivia as Stan and most people had always assumed. The girls' fathers had been fundamentalist football fanatics.

Stan and Matty were struck dumb by the revelations and almost wept with disappointment. They went to the gents together and were both sick in the cubicles. They had to go home and 'come out' about the situation, but in the end their families supported them. On the morning the couples were ready to go down to Wembley, Stan found his front door had been painted royal blue, and Matty's door had been painted LFC red. This spooked both families because their long deceased warring grandfathers used to paint their teams' colours on the front doors when a Derby was due. The milk man deepened the mystery because he had passed both doors at 7.30 am, and when he passed those same doors ten minutes later, they had been painted, yet he had seen and heard no one on the doorsteps.

Despite the spooky goings-on the lads and lasses married anyway – and are still together, and their children are a mixture of reds and blues!